Brittany knew she should back away, but her body ignored her brain.

His lips were soft at first, then more demanding. The thrill of their mingling breaths roared through her like fire. The inhibitions that had become part of her being melted away and she kissed him back, letting the heat of him wash though her.

The unexpected hunger for him was primal, untamed. Her arms slid around his neck, pulling him closer as her body arched toward his.

When he had the good sense to pull away, her body went weak.

"Don't think the doctor would approve of this." His voice was a husky whisper.

"Probably not," she agreed, though it wasn't her physical health she was worried about but her inability to control her emotions where Cannon was concerned. It wasn't the time or the place. Likely not even the right man, no matter how right it felt right now.

"Good night, Detective."

"Good night, cowboy."

MIDNIGHT RIDER

JOANNA WAYNE

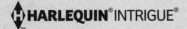

HARLEQUIN® INTRIGUE®

To my twin sisters, Linda and Brenda, and to all my readers from big families who know what it's like to love, chat, laugh, eat and sometimes cry with a houseful of siblings.

ISBN-13: 978-0-373-74860-0

Midnight Rider

Copyright © 2015 by Jo Ann Vest

Recycling programs for this product may not exist in your area.

This edition published by arrangement with Harlequin Books S.A.

For questions and comments about the quality of this book, please contact us at CustomerService@Harlequin.com.

Printed in U.S.A.

www.Harlequin.com

Joanna Wayne began her professional writing career in 1994. Now, more than fifty published books later, Joanna has gained a worldwide following with her cutting-edge romantic suspense and Texas family series such as Sons of Troy Ledger and the Big "D" Dads series. Joanna currently resides in a small community north of Houston, Texas, with her husband. You may write Joanna at PO Box 852, Montgomery, Texas 77356, or connect with her at joannawayne.com.

Books by Joanna Wayne

Harlequin Intrigue

Sons of Troy Ledger

Cowboy Swagger

Genuine Cowboy

AK-Cowboy

Cowboy Fever

Cowboy Conspiracy

Big "D" Dads

Son of a Gun

Live Ammo

Big Shot

Big "D" Dads: The Daltons

Trumped Up Charges

Unrepentant Cowboy

Hard Ride to Dry Gulch

Midnight Rider

Visit the Author Profile page at Harlequin.com for more titles

CAST OF CHARACTERS

Cannon Dalton—A bull rider and R. J. Dalton's youngest son.

Brittany "Brit" Garner—Houston homicide detective whom someone wants dead.

Sylvie Hamm—Brit's twin sister and Kimmie's mother.

Rick Drummond—Brit's partner.

Carla Bradford—Brit's supervisor who plays by the rules.

Clive Austin—A criminal capable of anything.

Melanie Crouch—Recently released from prison.

Marcus and Joyce Dalton—Brit's deceased parents.

Aidan McIntosh—Marcus's best friend, before Marcus was instrumental in sending Aidan to prison.

Louise McIntosh—Aidan's unforgiving wife.

R. J. Dalton—The owner of Dry Gulch Ranch, a dying father attempting to reconnect with his estranged adult children.

The rest of the Dalton family—

Adam Dalton, rancher; his wife, Hadley; their twin daughters, Lila and Lacy.

Leif Dalton, attorney; his veterinarian wife, Joni; and his teenage daughter, Effie.

Travis Dalton, Dallas homicide detective; his wife, Faith; and her teenage son, Cornell.

Jade Dalton, R.J.'s youngest daughter, still estranged.

Jake Dalton, R.J.'s oldest son, still estranged.

Chapter One

Brit Garner woke to the irritating rattle of her cell phone vibrating against her bedside table. She pulled the pillow over her head and tried to ignore it. It finally stopped only to start again a few seconds later. If this was her partner, she was going to kill him.

She checked the caller ID and then took the call. "This had better be of life-threatening importance, Rick Drummond."

"Not life threatening, but I think you better get down to the morgue."

"What part of 'I'm on vacation with plans to sleep until noon every day' do you not understand?"

"I get it. You've worked your gorgeous butt off the past few months. But I think you'll want to see this."

"I've seen dead bodies before." Too many of them, which was why she needed a few well-deserved days off. A walk in a park or along the beach would do wonders for her state of mind. Time to read a book or visit friends would be heaven.

Her dad had warned her it would be like this.

"Just come down. No work involved. I really think you should see this."

"Why is it so urgent I see this particular body?"

"Just get down here, Brit. I'll buy you coffee and breakfast after."

"A real breakfast. No coffee and doughnut on the fly."

"Anything you want—under ten bucks, of course."

"Splurging and secrecy. You're starting to freak me out. I'll be there as soon as I can throw on some clothes. Not work clothes. I'm on vacation, remember?"

"Hard to forget when you keep bringing it up every ten seconds. Come on up to Autopsy when you get here."

Brit kicked off the top sheet and stretched her legs over the side of the bed. She went to the bathroom, splashed her face with cold water and brushed her teeth. After that she shed her nightshirt and wiggled into a pair of faded jeans and a long-sleeved green T-shirt. A quick brush of her long hair and she was ready.

She'd go to the morgue but, no matter how

interesting the case, she wouldn't let Rick sway her to jump in. She really needed the time off. And not only to rejuvenate, but also to try to figure out where she'd gone wrong on a very important case.

The colder a case got the harder it was to solve. She'd been working on her father's murder for three years without a decent lead. She had to be overlooking a key element. No murder was perfect.

Less than a half hour later, she was walking into the autopsy section of the morgue. The facilities were state-of-the-art and as familiar as her neighborhood grocery store, though the odors were far more unpleasant.

Her partner, Rick, was standing next to the gray examining table. Her favorite pathologist, Elise Laughton, was at the other side of the table and slipping out of her gloves.

"Looks like she put up a hell of a fight," Elise said. "Evidently she was just no match for the strength of her attacker."

"Cause of death?" Brit asked by way of greeting, determined to stick to the basics.

"You made good time," Elise said, looking up.

"Traffic was light. And as you can see, I didn't bother with makeup since I'm not sticking around long."

Elise shared a concerned look with Rick and

then looked back to her. "To answer your original question, the evidence includes new bruising on the hands and arms and having her throat slashed."

Another morning in Houston. Not that all murders weren't bad, but any detective in the department could handle this, including Rick. There had to be something more going on for him to call her in this morning.

"So start talking, Rick, and this had better be good."

Rick frowned. "Take a look."

Brit stepped closer for an unobstructed view of the body. An icy chill seeped deep inside her as she studied the victim.

She could have been staring into a mirror. The lifeless victim spread out on the cold metal slab looked exactly like her.

Chapter Two

One Week Later

"How about passing that potato salad before Leif goes back for seconds and doesn't leave any for the rest of us?" Travis joked.

"Look who's talking," Leif said as he handed down the serving bowl. "You've been hogging the platter of fried chicken like a starving man."

"That's 'cause I had him out baling hay all afternoon," Adam said. "Nothing like a little ranch work to build up an appetite."

"Save room for the apple pie à la mode," Hadley said. "I made it myself and I'll be insulted if there's a bite left on a dish."

"Ice cream!" four-year-old Lacy added. She pushed her plate back. "I want mine now."

"Me, too," R.J. said, "but I better clean my plate first. You better eat a few more bites of dinner, too."

R.J. smiled and leaned back in his chair.

There was a time not so many months ago that he'd have been sitting at this table all alone. Or passed out somewhere skunk drunk. Now he was alcohol-free, thankful to be surrounded by family. Best medicine in the world for a dying man.

He didn't have much of an appetite these days, even though his daughters-in-law Hadley and Faith had become dadgum good cooks. His third daughter-in-law, Joni, was too busy being the best dang vet in the state of Texas to spend much time in the kitchen.

Besides, he suspected she might be pregnant. She'd turned green and rushed away from the breakfast table a couple of days ago and she'd developed a little swell in the belly. He wouldn't ask. She'd tell them all when she was ready.

It had been over a year now since the neurosurgeon had given R.J. the death sentence. A malignant, inoperable brain tumor that would eventually take his life. For some miraculous reason, the tumor had decided to slow down a bit and give R.J. time to enjoy his family—the family he'd never bothered to get to know when he was drinking and carousing like the SOB he'd been for most of his life.

He'd given little thought to contacting his estranged kids until the grim reaper had looked him square in the eye and chuckled. But getting to know Adam, Leif and Travis and their families had given his life more meaning than he'd thought possible. Why, already there had been three weddings on the Dry Gulch Ranch. Fortunately, none of them his. Four weddings were enough for any one man.

Still, with each passing day, the longing grew stronger to connect with his other three children. So far, no luck there. His youngest son, Cannon, was either too resentful or too busy with his bull riding to give R.J. the time of day.

His daughter, Jade, was the baby of the family, though she was in her early twenties now. The only times he'd seen her was when she came to the ranch for the reading of the will. She hadn't cared much for his requirement that a beneficiary would have to spend a year living on and helping work the Dry Gulch Ranch to get a share in his estate. Hadn't seemed too pleased that he'd had the reading of the will while he was still breathing, either.

Had let him know it, too, in no uncertain terms. As feisty a hellcat as her mother had been. The ranch had never offered enough excitement for Kiki. Apparently it didn't for their daughter, Jade, either.

And that left his oldest son, Jake, rich Texas rancher and oilman. The wealth inherited from his mother's side of the family. Jake had everything a man could want. Fancy cars. Private jets. Gorgeous women half his age draped across him in every picture of him that appeared on the society pages of the *Dallas Morning News*.

Jake had moved on so far he couldn't even see R.J. in his mind's rearview mirror. No doubt his mother had done the same. Stupidest mistake R.J. had ever made was letting her walk away. He wondered what she was like now. He still pictured her as young and beautiful as she'd been at eighteen when they'd married. Best-looking girl in the small country high school they'd attended. Hell, she was probably the best-looking girl in all of Texas back then.

The doorbell rang.

"Are you expecting company tonight?" Faith asked.

"Nope," R.J. said. "Probably a neighbor stopping by."

"I'll get it," Adam offered, already scooting back from the table.

"You just keep eatin'," R.J. said. "I need a little exercise. Old bones get stiff if I sit too long."

He held on to the edge of the table for extra support as he stood. Never knew when one of those dizzy spells would hit. He ambled to the door, taking his time about it. The doorbell rang again.

"Hold your horses. I'm coming."

He swung open the door and stared into the bluest eyes he'd ever seen. He took in the rest of the stranger, enjoying the tour. He might be near dead. But just because he couldn't sample the wares didn't mean he couldn't window-shop.

"You must be lost," he said, sure he'd never seen the tall, willowy strawberry blonde before.

"Is this the Dry Gulch Ranch?"

"Was the last time I looked at the sign over the gate."

"Are you R.J. Dalton?"

"Yep. You're batting a thousand so far."

"Then I'm not lost."

A baby whimpered.

R.J. followed the sound to a baby carrier resting on the porch, next to the stranger's right foot. The young woman reached down and grabbed the handle, lifting the carrier so that he could see the adorable infant peeking from beneath a yellow blanket. The baby kicked and made a few boxing moves with its tiny fists.

"And who might this be?" R.J. asked.

"This is your three-month-old granddaughter, Kimmie."

"My granddaughter. Well, don't that just beat all?"

"Yes, it does." She pushed the carrier toward him. When he didn't take it, she set it on the floor inside the door.

"Come on in," R.J. urged, opening the door even wider.

"No, thank you. I'm just here to drop off Kimmie."

"What do you mean drop her off?"

"Just that. I'm leaving her in your care."

"You can't do that. I'm a sick man. I can't take care of a baby." Had never done that when he was young and healthy.

"Then I suggest you hire someone to take care of her or call your son Cannon and tell him to stop by and pick up his daughter."

So Cannon was playing around with more than bulls. A chip off the old block. But the old block had made a lifetime of mistakes.

"Why don't you go tell Cannon that yourself?"

"I don't have time at the moment to go chasing down some irresponsible bull rider."

Apparently not time to raise her child, either.

She pulled a business card and an envelope from her pocket. "If Cannon has questions, he can reach me at this number. Inside the envelope, you'll find everything you need to know about caring for Kimmie."

"I'm gonna need a lot more than some notes."

"Yes, you'll need this to get you started." The woman slid a large canvas tote from her shoulder and handed it to him, as well. "There's formula, bottles, diapers and a few changes of clothing inside."

"You got a momma for her in there, too?"

The woman didn't answer, but he could swear those striking blue eyes of hers were moist when she turned and walked away.

She stopped just before she reached her car. "I play classical music for Kimmie when she gets fussy. It calms her down."

There was a definite quiver in her voice but no hesitation as she got into her car and drove away.

Once her taillights disappeared, R.J. took a look at the card she'd pressed into his left hand. *Brittany Garner, Homicide Detective, Houston Police Department.*

Cannon sure knew how to pick them. Gorgeous, sexy and she could handle a weapon. *All good traits in a woman—unless she turned the gun on you.*

R.J. was still staring at the newest addition to the family when his daughter-in-law Hadley joined him at the door. She stopped and stared at the baby. "Oh, my gosh. Look how adorable."

Hadley reached down, unbuckled the baby from her chair and picked her up, all the while gushing baby talk.

"Hello, little sweetie. Did you just drop from heaven and land at our door?"

"Something like that," R.J. said.

Hadley's eyebrows arched. She dropped the baby talk. "What are you talking about? Who is this?"

"Name's Kimmie, or so her mother said."

"Who's her mother?"

"Apparently a lady cop."

"What do you mean apparently? You must know whose baby this is?" Hadley walked to the door and looked out. "Where is her mom?"

"Gone back to Houston, I s'pect."

"Without her baby? What's going on here?"

"Supposedly this is my granddaughter."

"Who's the father?"

"Allegedly, it's Cannon, but I bet he's gonna be as surprised about this as we are."

R.J. smiled in spite of the situation. Not the ideal bargaining tool, but it was one way to get Cannon back to the Dry Gulch Ranch. His neighbor Caroline Lambert was right. God sure worked in mysterious ways.

Chapter Three

Macabre kicked his way out of the creaky gate with a vengeance that sent adrenaline exploding through Cannon's veins.

One. Two.

The bull bucked wildly. The rope dug into Cannon's gloved hand. His lucky Stetson went flying. Bad omen.

Three. Four.

The crowd's cheers mingled with the thunderous stamping of the bull's hooves and the frantic beating of Cannon's heart.

Five.

Cannon's body shifted and began to slide. Instinct took over. He struggled to hang on, leaning hard, fighting to shift his weight.

Macabre's fierce back hooves propelled the animal's powerful muscles, twisting and spinning the two-ton mass of fury. The rope slipped. White-hot pain ripped through Cannon's shoulder.

He was on the ground. The rank breath of the snorting bull burned in his own nostrils. Flying dirt blinded him. He blinked, covered his head with his hands and rolled away.

Shouts from the rodeo clown echoed though the arena, but the bull didn't back off. It swerved and came back at Cannon.

Cannon rolled in the opposite direction. The crowd gasped in unison as one hoof came so close to his head that Cannon could feel the vibrations rattle inside his skull.

Then the bull turned and went after the clown. Cannon owed Billy Cox big-time.

He picked himself up, grabbed his hat and waved it to the crowd as he scrambled back to safety. Cox was safe, as well. Only then did Cannon check the results.

Seven seconds.

Disappointment burned inside him. One more second and he would have scored big. He'd drawn Macabre, the most vicious of the bulls on tonight's docket. The animal that could have put Cannon in pay dirt.

Already December, one of the last of the rodeos in what had been a great year for Cannon. Still, he could have used that prize money. Like most rodeo addicts who loved bull riding, the day would come when he'd have to retire. He'd need *mucho* cash to do that right.

What was a cowboy without a ranch?

"Bad luck," one of the other riders said.

"I'd say good luck," another said. "You could have been leaving here in an ambulance tonight."

"Seven seconds on Macabre should be worth ten on any of the other bulls in the chute tonight."

Cannon acknowledged the comments with a nod and a shrug. Nothing else was needed. They all knew the disappointment of losing to a bull.

"Mighty tough way to make a living."

The voice was unfamiliar, gruff, but with a rattle that came with lots of years of living. Cannon turned to see who'd spoken.

Reality sent a shot of acid straight to his gut. As if tonight hadn't already been bad enough.

"What are you doing here?" Cannon asked.

"I came to see my son ride," R.J. said. "No law against that, is there?"

Probably should be. "You've seen me," Cannon said. "Now what?"

"We need to talk," R.J. said.

Cannon wasn't interested in pretending he had any fatherly feelings for a man who hadn't given a damn about him when he could have used his help. And he wouldn't play any part in the old man's search for redemption before he died.

Actually, he'd figured R.J. was already dead by now. Or maybe everything he'd said about the inoperable brain tumor at the bizarre reading of his will had been lies. He wouldn't put anything past R.J. Dalton.

"I know you have no use for me," R.J. continued. "I probably deserve that. We still need to talk. And I have someone you should meet."

"Look, R.J., you had your say at the reading of your will. I wasn't interested then. I'm still not. I don't play games."

"Looks like you were playing a potentially deadly one tonight."

"That's work, not a game. And it's my business."

"So is what I have to tell you."

"Then spit it out."

"Okay. You think I'm a lousy father. I agree. But unless I miss my guess, you're about to get the chance to prove you're a hundred times better at it than I ever was."

"I don't know what you're talking about."

"You will in a minute. Come with me."

Crazy old fool. Cannon couldn't even begin to guess what kind of absurd scheme he was working now. He leaned against the wooden railing that separated the contenders from the rest of the arena as R.J. ambled off without looking back.

Every muscle in his body complained silently, aches and pain seeping in like the bitter cold of a West Texas winter morning. He craved a hot shower, a couple of over-the-counter painkillers with a six-pack to wash them down.

Then he'd plop on the lumpy mattress back at the motel. No place like home, and a lonely motel room was as close to home as he'd been since he'd finished his tour of duty with the marines.

But something had brought R.J. clear out to Abilene to talk to Cannon. Doubtful the old coot would just turn around and drive home without saying whatever he'd come to say. Might as well get it over with.

Cannon followed in the direction R.J. had gone. He spotted him a couple of minutes later, standing near the wooden bleachers. A stunning young woman stood next to him, cuddling a baby in her arms.

Surely R.J. didn't have the testosterone to father another child at his age. And even if he had, why would he think Cannon would give a damn?

The woman turned toward him and attempted a smile that didn't quite work. Her gaze shifted from him back to the sleeping baby.

R.J.'s words about his getting a chance to prove himself as a father echoed through his mind. If he thought Cannon was going to raise this baby for him he was nuts. So was the infant's mother.

A more troublesome angle struck him. Surely, R.J. wasn't insinuating Cannon could have fathered this baby.

He studied the woman. Fiery red hair that cascaded around her shoulders. Deep green eyes. Not a woman a man could easily forget, yet she didn't stir any memories for him.

"I'm Hadley Dalton," she said as he approached. "Your half brother Adam's wife. And this is Kimmie." She held up the baby for him to get a better look. The infant stretched and rubbed her eyes with her tiny balled fists, but then settled back to sleep.

So this was Adam's child. Cannon exhaled, releasing the dread and the breath he hadn't realized he'd been holding. "Cute baby. You and Adam did well."

"But that's just the thing," R.J. said. "It's not their baby. You're her dad, or at least some woman down in Houston claims you are."

Macabre's hooves couldn't have packed a bigger wallop.

Chapter Four

Cannon took a long swig of the cold beer. It did nothing to ease the shock or to relieve the aches in his joints and muscles. R.J. and Hadley sat across the booth from him in the nearby café where they'd gone to finish their discussion. The infant slept in Hadley's arms.

The confusion he'd felt back at the arena was growing worse instead of better. "I don't even know anyone named Brittany Garner. I definitely didn't have a child with her. She evidently has me confused with someone else."

"She seemed pretty sure about her facts when she dropped Kimmie off with us," R.J. said.

"She could be just trying to get money out of *you*," Cannon said. "If she knows anything at all about me, she knows I'm not worth conning."

"She's a detective," Hadley offered. "Surely she wouldn't be working a con."

"Anyone can have business cards printed," Cannon said. "That doesn't prove she's a cop."

"She's a cop all right," R.J. assured him. "Your half brother Travis is a homicide detective himself in Dallas. He had her checked out. She's legit and apparently good at her job."

She might be a detective, but Cannon wasn't convinced he'd slept with her. "How old is this woman?"

"Looks to be in her late twenties," R.J. said. "'Bout your age. Sky-blue eyes. Tall. Thin. Strawberry-blond hair. Damned good-looking if that helps jog your memory."

It didn't. "Awful young for a detective," Cannon commented, not that it mattered. He was twenty-seven himself and he'd already finished a stint with the marines and made a name for himself on the rodeo circuit.

"How old is Kimmie?" he asked.

"Three months, according to Brit Garner," R.J. said.

Cannon went over the basics in his mind. Kimmie was three months old. This was the first week in December. If Kimmie was his, she would have been conceived about a year ago. That would have meant he had to be in Houston last December.

The big Houston Livestock Show and Rodeo was always in March. He'd participated in that, but didn't recall being in Houston any other time. Of course, he might have passed through on his way to somewhere else. He'd have to check his calendar.

He wasn't into one-night stands, but that didn't mean he'd never given in to temptation. He definitely hadn't been in a relationship then, or any time in recent memory. Have a few good times with a woman and she was ready to pick out furniture and run your life.

A one-nighter with a gorgeous Houston detective that he didn't remember. Extremely unlikely.

"You can get a paternity test," Hadley said. "That's the only way you can know for sure if you're Kimmie's father."

"A paternity test." He sounded like a nervous parrot. But he couldn't even begin to wrap his head around the possibility that the baby sleeping in Hadley's arms could be his.

"I hear they're easy to get these days," R.J. agreed. "If you're short of cash, I can front you the money."

"I'm not the father," Cannon insisted, but his stomach had twisted into a huge, gnarly knot.

Kimmie began to stir. She stretched and yawned and then tried to poke her entire fist into her wide-open mouth. Hadley moved her to her other shoulder, but the baby continued to fuss.

"She's hungry," Hadley said. "Would you like

to hold her, Cannon, while I get her bottle from the diaper bag?"

Hold that squirming ball of life? Not a chance. A puppy, he could handle. But this was a real live baby.

"I wouldn't know how," he said.

"I s'pect you better learn," R.J. said. "Not only how to hold her, but also how to feed her and change her and even bathe her—that is, if she turns out to be yours."

R.J. was already a believer. Cannon could tell by that knowing look in his eyes even though his pupils were half-hidden by the bags beneath them and the loose skin that drooped over his lids.

Kimmie started to cry. Cannon's muscles bunched. The prospect of fatherhood struck him with raw fear, the kind of paralyzing fright he'd never felt when climbing atop a bull.

"Maybe you should stay at the Dry Gulch Ranch while you have the paternity testing done," Hadley suggested. "There's plenty of room since R.J. is the only one actually living in the original ranch house now. The rest of us have built our own houses on the Dry Gulch now.

"I'd be close enough to help you with Kimmie if you're at the ranch, but I can't stay here.

Adam and I have two young daughters of our own who need me."

Stay at the Dry Gulch and then owe his worthless biological father for the favor. The prospect was repulsive. But what other options did he have? He couldn't walk out of here tonight with a baby in his arms and no idea how to care for her.

He had six days before his next rodeo, time he needed to get over his sore shoulder. But what if the paternity test proved it was his baby. Then what? Drag Kimmie around in a saddle blanket?

The baby had a mother. Detective or not, she'd have to take over the parenting chores until the kid was old enough to at least tell Cannon why she was crying.

Great attitude. If he wasn't careful he'd rival R.J. for the Worst Father of a Lifetime award.

Cannon finished his beer while Hadley fed the baby. "How many times a day do you have to do that?"

"About every four hours during the day. Kimmie has a healthy appetite. She goes longer between feedings at night."

"She takes a bottle at night, too?"

"She sleeps through most of the night but wakes up around five in the morning for a feeding. The good news is she goes right back to sleep after that, and usually doesn't wake up again until about eight."

No wonder the mystery detective was ready to hand the infant off to him. She was probably sleep deprived. Only what kind of mother would trust a man like him with their child?

Either Detective Brittany Garner had no idea what he was like or she was one totally irresponsible mother.

"I need to go to Houston and talk to Detective Garner," he said. "I hate to ask, Hadley, but if you'd watch Kimmie just for another day or two, until I can get the paternity test and sort all this out, I'd really appreciate it."

"You want me to take her back to the Dry Gulch Ranch?"

"Just for a few days."

"I can manage that."

"But no more than a few days," R.J. cautioned. "If Kimmie turns out to be your biological daughter, then she's your responsibility. Yours and the mother who dropped her off like a stray kitten."

R.J. was a fine one to give advice on parenting. Cannon was willing to bet he'd never in his life changed a diaper or gotten up at five in the morning to poke a bottle at a crying infant.

If the test came back positive—which he was almost certain it wouldn't—Cannon would at least make a stab at being a dad. There had to be a book that would help.

Sure, parenting by the book. About like a guidebook could teach a man how to stay on a mad, bucking bull for eight seconds.

"Are you driving back to Dallas tonight?" Cannon asked.

"We're flying back," R.J. said. "Tague Lambert, one of our neighbors, flew us down in his private jet. He's waiting at the small airport just west of town."

"So if you'll just take Kimmie with you, I'll drive to the ranch when I finish my business with Brit Garner," Cannon reiterated.

"You can fly back with us," R.J. offered. "Get the testing done in Dallas, might even be able to schedule it for tomorrow. Then you can wait until you have the facts to contact Kimmie's mother. You can use one of the vehicles at the ranch to take care of business."

"I don't go anywhere without my pickup truck," Cannon said, dismissing the offer. The less time he spent around R.J. the better.

The conversation dried up and died while his mind searched for reasons this baby couldn't be his and why some woman was trying to screw him over.

Once Kimmie had her fill and spit the nipple from her tiny, heart-shaped lips, Hadley set the almost empty nursing bottle on the table and shifted the baby in her arms. "Don't you want to at least hold her and say hello before we go?"

Cannon shook his head, though he figured it made him look like a jerk. "I've never held a baby before. I'm afraid I'd do it wrong and hurt her."

"You won't." Hadley stood and walked to his side of the booth. "Stand up and hold out your arms. I'll show you how to cradle her."

He stood, but kept his arms to his sides. "I don't think I should…."

"Nonsense." Hadley handed the baby off to him.

He took her reluctantly, standing stiffly while she fit the baby into his arms.

Kimmie's eyes fluttered, eyes the same general color as his, only lighter. Cannon's breath caught in his throat.

The infant was practically weightless, but not still. She squirmed and started to fuss as if she knew he didn't have a clue what he was doing. At least she was smart.

Cannon touched her chin with a fingertip. Her skin was as soft as silk. She made a gurgling noise and kicked and swung her little arms like a wind-up toy.

Her short, chubby fingers somehow caught and wrapped around the one he'd used to touch her cheek. An emotion he didn't recognize shot through him and settled in his heart.

He had never been more afraid in his life.

BY THE TIME Cannon returned to his hotel room, the shock had worn off enough that the aches and pains had checked back in. He headed straight for a shower, shedding his clothes as he went. For the first time he noticed the rip in his jeans and the dirt stains blotching his Western shirt.

Stripped naked by the time he reached the bathroom, he glanced in the mirror. The area around his rib cage was already turning an ugly shade of purple.

Macabre was no doubt sleeping comfortably in his stall, probably dreaming of what he'd do to the next sucker crazy enough to climb on his back.

Cannon turned the knobs on the shower until the spray was steamy hot. He stepped in and let the water sluice over his head and run down his aching body.

He closed his eyes, but the relief he'd hoped for didn't come. Instead, an image of Kimmie rocked his mind. Could she possibly be his daughter? He racked his brain trying to remember his schedule for last December.

Nothing stood out. His life was a steady

stream of rodeos and towns he barely saw except for the arenas where the action took place. After years on the circuit, they ran together like gravy ladled over a plate of biscuits and sausage.

He remembered the big events. Dallas. Austin. Houston. San Antonio. Phoenix. Las Vegas. Hell, he even made it up to Montana on occasion. It all depended on the points he needed and how big the purse was.

There had been women. Not that many, but a few. Never married ones, at least not knowingly. And he stayed clear of the underage buckle bunnies who hung around the arenas and flirted shamelessly with any cowboy who'd give them the time of day. Plenty did. They could get a man in big trouble.

More to the point, he kept a supply of condoms handy—just in case.

The way he saw it, there was damned little chance that Kimmie was his daughter.

So why had he felt that quake deep in his gut when Kimmie had accidentally latched on to his finger? Couldn't be because he had some kind of secret longing to father a child.

He had his future all planned out. His winnings from the rodeo were his ticket to making it happen. A kid would put the skids on his dreams faster than a bull could clear the chute.

He should call Brittany Garner tonight and tell her she had the wrong man.

No. Better to see her face-to-face. If he had sex with her, he'd surely remember her once he was looking at her. If he'd been sober enough to get it up, then his brain cells should have been functioning at least at a minuscule level.

He soaped his body, gingerly, especially over the bruised flesh. Then he rinsed and stepped out of the shower. He grabbed one of the bleached white towels from the shelf and wrapped it around his waist.

The dull pounding at the base of his skull that had been playing background drums for him ever since the fall intensified. He took the bottle of extrastrength painkillers from his duffel and shook two into his left hand. He swallowed them with a chaser of water he'd cupped in his hand from the faucet.

Rummaging in his shaving duffel, he dug out a toothbrush and squeezed a roll of minty jell along the bristles. The brushing did little to rid his mouth of the coppery taste that had taken hold the second he'd learned he might be a father.

Fatigue stitched with dread settled in hard as he walked to the bed, dropped his towel to the floor and threw back the heavy spread. Tomorrow he'd make the long drive to Houston. Tonight he had to get some rest.

Sleep came almost instantly. Unfortunately, it didn't last. By four in the morning, Cannon was behind the wheel of his pickup truck, pulling out of the hotel parking lot. Brit Garner's business card was deep in his pocket.

Talk was cheap, especially from a detective who admittedly slept around. A paternity test was all it would take to prove that she was wrong.

THE CLERK AT the police precinct stared at Cannon, her gaze focused on the angry raw scrape that colored his right cheek. "Are you here to file an assault complaint?"

"No. I'm here to see Detective Brittany Garner. Is she in?"

"The detective is with someone in her office now. What's your business with her?"

"Personal."

The middle-aged clerk leveled her gaze, her features hardening as if she suddenly found his visit threatening or just downright annoying. "Detective Garner is very busy, but give me your name and I'll see if she has time to see you."

"Cannon Dalton and she'll see me."

The clerk rolled her eyes at him as if he was just another nuisance in her day. "Wait here."

The wait was short. The clerk returned less than a minute later. "The detective will see you now. I'll walk you to her office."

He followed the clerk down a narrow corridor, taking a left at the end of the hall. She opened a door and motioned him to go in.

R.J.'s description hadn't done the stunning woman behind the desk justice. She did look vaguely familiar, but damned if he could place her. Probably reminded him of some movie star or supermodel. She had the body and the looks for either one.

"I'm glad you finally found time to stop by, Mr. Dalton. We need to talk." Her voice was stern, her manner stiffly authoritative. All cop. Not quite what he'd expected from a woman who was about to say, *Hey, guess what? I had your baby.*

Maybe Kimmie wasn't her daughter, after all. But surely the Houston Police Department didn't have the staff to send homicide detectives out to find deadbeat dads.

Cannon let his gaze travel over her while she slid some loose papers into a brown envelope. Striking eyes, the color of a summer sky. Hair was shiny and straight and fell past her shoulders. Long bangs were tucked behind her left ear.

Finally she sat down and told him to do the

same. He settled in the straight-backed metal chair across from her desk. He looked her in the eye. Hers were accusing. They matched her smug expression.

"I'm glad you stopped by. This will be much easier to deal with in person."

"Might have been easier if you'd talked to me before you dumped your kid on R.J.'s doorstep."

"I didn't dump. I *delivered* Kimmie to her grandfather since her father wasn't around to accept responsibility for her welfare."

"Part of your official duties as a detective?"

"As a matter of fact, it was."

"And how did you reach the conclusion that I'm Kimmie's father?"

"Maybe I should refresh your memory."

"You definitely should."

"Marble Falls, Texas. Last December. The Greenleaf Bar. Does that mean anything to you?"

Marble Falls. Last December. A resort-sponsored rodeo. He groaned as the pieces started to fall together.

"The woman in Greenleaf Bar was you?"

"You don't remember?"

"Vaguely."

He struggled to put things in perspective. That had been a hell of a night. He'd stopped at the first bar he'd come to after leaving the rodeo.

A blonde had sat down next to him. As best he remembered, he'd given her an earful about the rodeo, life and death as he'd become more and more inebriated.

She must have offered him a ride back to his hotel since his truck had still been at the bar when he'd gone looking for it the next morning. If Brit was telling the truth, the woman must have gone into the motel with him and they'd ended up doing the deed.

If so, he'd been a total jerk. She'd been as drunk as him and driven or she'd willingly taken a huge risk.

Hard to imagine the woman staring at him now ever being that careless or impulsive.

"Is that your normal pattern, Mr. Dalton?" Brit asked "Use a woman to satisfy your physical needs and then ride off to the next rodeo?"

"That's a little like the armadillo calling the squirrel road kill, isn't it? I'm sure I didn't coerce you into my bed if I was so drunk I can't remember the experience."

"I can assure you that you're nowhere near that irresistible. I have never been in your bed."

"Whew. That's a relief. I'd have probably died of frostbite."

"This isn't a joking matter."

"I'm well aware. But I'm not the enemy here, so you can quit talking to me like I just climbed out from under a slimy rock. If you're not Kimmie's mother, who is?"

"My twin sister, Sylvie Hamm."

Twin sisters. That explained Brit's attitude. Probably considered her sister a victim of the drunken sex urges he didn't remember. It also explained why Brit Garner looked familiar.

"So why is it I'm not having this conversation with Sylvie?"

"She's dead."

The words sank in slowly, changing everything. "I'm sorry," he said honestly. The how and why of all of this seemed less important now. A baby would grow up never knowing her mother. A baby that might be his.

He tried to wrap his mind around the new development. The death had to be recent. Kimmie was just a baby. "How did your sister die?"

"She was murdered."

A new jolt shook his system as the situation grew even more disturbing. He muttered a few careless curse words, not out of disrespect but out of desperation. He didn't see how things could get much worse, but from the look on Brit's face, he had a feeling they were about to.

"I get the feeling I should be calling in a lawyer about now," he said.

"Not if you have nothing to hide. You're not

currently a suspect in her murder, Mr. Dalton, if that's what you're thinking."

Currently the operative word. "Have you arrested a suspect?" he asked.

"Not yet."

"Do you have one?"

"No."

"A motive?"

"It's an open investigation. I can't really discuss the details with you."

"Exactly what can you share, Detective?"

Brit stood and walked around to the front of her desk, propping her shapely backside on the edge of it. Hard-edged, probably tough as nails, but hard to get past the fact that she looked more like a starlet playing a cop than an actual detective. There had to be a story there somewhere.

"What specifically would you like to know, Mr. Dalton?"

"First, how about calling me Cannon? If I am Kimmie's father, then we're practically related."

"Okay, what do you want to know, Cannon?"

"For starters, why would you hand over your niece to a man like R.J. Dalton, or to me, for that matter, since you think I'm such a lowlife?"

She hesitated, then exhaled slowly as if she were giving in against her better judgment. "I'd planned to take that up with you after we have the results of the paternity test in hand, but since you're so eager to discuss details, I guess we can talk now."

"Then we finally agree on something."

Brit glanced at her watch. "Do you mind if we talk over a sandwich? I haven't eaten since breakfast and I need some food and decent coffee."

"Fine by me, as long as I'm not riding to the restaurant in the back of a squad car."

Her full lips tipped into a slight smile. "Not this trip. There's an informal restaurant with quick service just around the corner. We can walk."

"Lead the way."

Actually he had few hunger pangs growling in his stomach, as well. He'd driven straight through, grabbing snacks for munching when he'd stopped for fuel and bathroom breaks.

Snippets of that night in Marble Falls kicked around in his mind as they walked to the café. He hated that his memories of that night were lost in a whiskey fog. Weird considering he wasn't even that much of a drinker. A beer or two every now and then. A six-pack on a bad night.

The night in Marble Falls had been far worse than bad.

Right now he figured he wasn't the only one with questions. And, in spite of Brit's assurances, he figured he was one wrong answer away from becoming a suspect.

That still didn't mean she had her facts right about his being Kimmie's father.

Chapter Five

So this was the rodeo cowboy Sylvie Hamm had found irresistible. Brit had to admit he wasn't the sort of a man who'd go unnoticed in a bar or most anywhere else.

His skin was tanned. His eyes were penetrating—caramel colored with gold flecks that made them almost hypnotizing when his gaze locked with hers. His hair was a sun-streaked brown, unruly, thick locks falling rakishly over his brow.

He needed a shave, but the rough growth of whiskers only added to his blatant masculinity, as did the angry, skinned blotch on his left cheek.

Worn jeans that fit to perfection, white Western shirt, sleeves rolled to the elbows. And a sauntering charisma and Texas drawl that left no doubt he was the real deal.

Put that package of screaming virility in a cozy bar with a steamy country ballad for background. A few drinks. A belly-rubbing dance or two. Then a burning kiss that rocked your soul…

Brit swallowed hard and shook the sensual images from her mind. Her relationship with Cannon Dalton was strictly business. She'd been angry with him since the day she'd learned that he was Kimmie's missing-in-action father.

But he was also the only link to Sylvie. Aggravating him or making him defensive would not help her cause. Sylvie could have said or done something the night they'd been together that would lead Brit to the killer. She also needed enough information to decide if he would be a fit father for Kimmie.

If not, biological rights or not, Brit would do whatever it took to keep him from getting custody of her niece.

That move would be a last resort. Brit knew more about the rodeo than she did about taking care of a baby—and that was absolutely nothing.

"Jodie's Grill and Deli. Is this the place?" Cannon asked as they approached the green awning that shielded the entrance from the elements.

"Yes. It's larger than it looks from the outside and mostly a lunch spot, so it shouldn't be too crowded tonight."

He hurried ahead to get the door. Their shoulders brushed as she stepped past him. A jolt of unexpected heat surged through her. She stepped away quickly.

What was it about this man that was getting to her?

"Would you like a booth or a table?" the hostess asked when they stepped inside.

"How about that back booth?" Cannon suggested, nodding to one that the busboy was wiping down.

"Certainly, sir."

"Okay with you, Brit?" he asked after the fact.

She nodded, surprised he'd called her by the shortened version of her first name. Rick was the only male in Homicide who did. To everyone else she was Garner.

It was as if she and Cannon had just skipped a few steps of the introductory stage. Perhaps part of the cowboy way, like his swagger and virility.

They followed the hostess past a cluster of occupied tables to the back corner of the dining area. Brit took the seat that let her see the door. It was a cop thing to always be able to watch and assess what was going on in any situation.

Cannon slid onto the padded bench seat opposite hers and opened his menu. "Any recommendations?" he asked as the hostess walked away.

"Salads are excellent," Brit said. "My favorite

is the Greek salad with a side of hummus and pita bread."

"You mean for starters?"

"No. They're large portions."

"To you, maybe. Show me the beef."

"In that case I hear their ribs and burgers are great."

"That's more like it."

When the waitress showed up, he ordered the rib platter with two sides and a beer on draft to wash it down.

Brit ordered her usual with coffee.

The waitress returned quickly with their drinks. Cannon took a hefty swig of the beer, wiped his mouth on the white cotton napkin and plunged right into the reason they were there.

"I enjoy a good mystery as much as the next guy, but not when I'm playing a supporting role. So let's get to the nitty-gritty of this. What makes you think I'm Kimmie's father?"

"I don't just think it. I'm reasonably certain. When we searched her apartment after Sylvie's murder, I found a file that contained a legal document that she'd downloaded from the internet. It wasn't notarized, but nonetheless, it was still clearly her intent that her written wishes be upheld."

"And this document mentioned me by name?"

"Yes. It specified that in the case of her death

or an injury that left her mentally or physically incapacitated, Cannon Dalton, the biological father of her daughter Kimmie, should be notified that he had a daughter."

"There must be more than one Cannon Dalton in Texas."

"Not one whose father owns the Dry Gulch Ranch."

"She put that in there, too?"

"Yes, either you told her the night she got pregnant or she did some research to make sure Kimmie ended up in the right hands."

"So you're just relying on a computer document that anyone could have printed out and Sylvie never mentioned my name to you while she was pregnant?"

"The form was filed with other important papers. I have no reason to believe it was false."

"Whose baby did you think she was carrying?" A husband's? A fiancé's? A current lover's?

"It's a very complicated situation, but the truth is I had never met Sylvie. I didn't even know she existed until she was murdered."

Brit stirred a packet of sweetener into her coffee and then took a sip before meeting Cannon's penetrating gaze.

"How is it you didn't know your twin sister?"

This was getting sticky. She'd rather not delve

into her personal life with Cannon. On the other hand, he was Kimmie's father. She had to tell him something.

Brit explained as succinctly as possible about being called to the morgue, glossing over how intensely disturbing it had been to see what looked like a waxed copy of herself laid out on the metal slab.

"A simple DNA test proved that we were twins," Brit said, "and that Sylvie was Kimmie's biological mother. By the time that was verified, I was neck-deep in the murder investigation."

"That's tough. I wish I could be more help," Cannon said, "but this came at me from out of the blue. Right now I'm drawing a blank about that night."

"I think the appropriate next step for you would be to have DNA testing to determine for certain that you are Kimmie's father."

"I agree. Any suggestions as to how to best go about that?"

"We have a lab here in town that handles the overflow from the police department. That would be the quickest bet. I can call now and find out if they can see you in the morning."

"Then let's get this rolling."

She made the call while Cannon finished his beer and worried the salt shaker with his free hand. She could easily understand his being disturbed by the news he was almost certainly a father.

Fortunately, the lab was able to accommodate.

"They'll see you at nine in the morning," she said once she'd broken the phone connection.

"Where is this lab?"

"Not far from here." She took a business card from her pocket and jotted down the street and web addresses of the lab on the back of the card before handing it to him. "You can get a map with directions at the website as well as pretest instructions about what you can and can't eat or drink before coming in."

"I can handle that. When will I get the results?"

"I'll request a rush, but it depends on how backed up they are at the lab. We should hear in about three days."

"That seems like long time for a rush."

"It's a very busy lab, but extremely reliable. You won't have to stay in Houston. They'll call you when the analysis is complete. Be sure to check the box on the form you sign for them that you want phone notification."

Cannon took another swig of beer, scrunched his napkin and then turned his attention back to Brit. "Once you suspected I was the father, why didn't you bring Kimmie to me instead of to the Dry Gulch Ranch? I don't live there now and never have."

"Your father was easier to locate."

"Wrong answer. You're a hotshot detective. You could have found me had you wanted to. I'm sure you checked out R.J. and me before you dropped off a helpless infant."

Right again. He wasn't as gullible as she'd expected and definitely not awed by her badge.

"I did investigate you, Cannon. You went into the Marines right out of high school. You list your uncle's ranch near Midland as your permanent address, but he said you haven't actually lived there in years. You have never been married and have no arrest record."

"That doesn't answer my question."

"I'm trying to find Sylvie's killer and I didn't have time to chase you down at a rodeo. And I wasn't about to leave my niece at a dirty arena with a bunch of sweaty cowboys and smelly livestock."

"Don't pretty it up on my account."

"I'm sorry. I know this is new, but this has all been rather shocking to me, as well. Once I learned that your father lived on a large ranch surrounded by family, I decided they could handle taking care of Kimmie and getting you in to see me."

"Fair enough, but if you disapprove of me and

my lifestyle so vehemently, why drop her off at all? You could have raised her yourself. I didn't know she existed."

"That would have been illegal and unethical once I found that document. Besides, I couldn't in good conscience ignore my sister's written wishes."

Not to mention that she'd tried caring for Kimmie and found it nearly impossible to work night and day on finding Sylvie's killer, work the rest of her cases and take on the extremely demanding job of taking care of an infant.

She couldn't begin to imagine how Cannon would handle it, but he was the father. He'd have to work out something.

"Where is Kimmie now?" Brit asked.

"At the Dry Gulch Ranch, but that's temporary. I don't have any ties with R.J. Dalton and I don't want him in my daughter's life—if I have a daughter. I'm far from convinced that I do, no matter what your sister wrote on some form."

"The DNA testing will settle that."

"It won't settle what I'm supposed to do with her if the test comes out positive. I can't take care of a baby. I don't even know where to start."

"Maybe you should have thought about that before you got my sister pregnant."

"If I'd been sober and thinking, she wouldn't

have gotten pregnant. And, contrary to what you infer, it takes two to tango. I don't push myself on women."

"That you remember."

Cannon emptied the glass of beer and set it down with a loud clunk. "I say we table the rest of this conversation until we know the results of the paternity test." He pulled his wallet from his pocket, took out a few bills and tossed them on the table, then stood to leave. "I'll be in touch."

"You haven't eaten yet."

"I'd prefer to eat where the air doesn't crackle with animosity."

She'd said too much. Her boss had warned her that if she gave her this case Brit would have to keep her emotions out of it. But she'd lost a sister she'd never gotten to meet, a sister who had left a precious baby behind.

The waitress arrived with the meal. Great timing. The overflowing plate of ribs, fries and coleslaw had an immediate effect on Cannon's demeanor.

"I'm sorry for the last comment," Brit said. "It was out of line. Stay and eat. Please."

Cannon sat back down and ordered another beer. After that, he gave the food his full attention.

Brit waited until he bit the remaining shred of

meat from the last rib before getting back down to business. This time she made sure to keep her tone nonaccusing.

"Can we start over?" Brit suggested.

He stared her down. "Will it make a difference?"

"Yes. If I could ask you a few questions, it might help with the investigation. I promise to maintain a civil tone."

"That would be worth seeing."

Brit did her best to put aside the irritation toward Cannon she'd been nursing for almost a week.

"I know you said you don't remember much about the evening you met my sister, Cannon, but if I ask you a few questions, maybe it will trigger a memory."

"Worth a try," he agreed. "I'd like to help you. No one deserves to be murdered, especially not a young mother minding her own business."

"Was Sylvie alone at the bar that night or with a friend?"

"I don't remember seeing her talking to anyone else. That doesn't mean she didn't come in with someone."

"Did she mention a boyfriend, maybe one that she was supposed to meet there or had recently broken up with?"

He shook his head. "Not that I remember."

"Did she seem afraid or talk about being afraid?"

He hesitated, his facial expression grim as if he really was attempting to remember a useful detail.

"I'm sorry. I was dealing with some heavy stuff of my own that night. All I remember about your sister is that she was there, drinking beer and putting up with me. I'm not proud of this, but to be totally honest, I don't even remember her being in the hotel with me."

"Then she wasn't still in the room when you woke up?"

"No. *That* I would have remembered. Did you question the bartender and waitresses who work there to see if they knew her?"

"I questioned everyone," Brit said. "No one remembered either of you. But then it has been a year. Some had moved on to other jobs, some to other parts of the country."

Cannon shifted in his seat, looked around until he caught their waitress's eye and signaled for a check. Obviously he was eager to escape her and her questions.

She wouldn't push further tonight. Cannon was probably too bogged down with worrying

over the paternity test results to think about anything else.

Brit was convinced the test results would be
positive. Whether or not that was a good thing
remained to be seen. But she had to admit that
she could see why Sylvie had felt an immediate
attraction to the sexy cowboy. He was a virile,
rough and tough bull rider with a Texas drawl
and a piercing stare that could shake a woman
to her soul.

Some women. Not Brit, of course.

By THE TIME Cannon reached his hotel, he was
dead tired and ready to crash. Even so, he
doubted sleep would come quick or last long.
He'd received bad news on top of bad news over
the past twenty-four hours and the hits just kept
coming.

The murder of a lover he didn't even remember being in bed with. A gorgeous homicide cop
who thought of him as a disgusting rodeo bum.

A baby who'd curled her short, stubby finger around his callused one. His heart twisted
inside him at the memory. But it didn't change
anything. Definitely didn't mean he could give
Kimmie what she needed.

Brit surely realized that. Or maybe not. He'd
never been good at figuring out women. Brit
was even thornier to figure than most.

She had an intensity about her that most of the young buckle bunnies who hung around the arena in their short shorts, bulging cleavage and ready temptation lacked. But then she was older than most of them and a homicide detective.

The kind of woman who either irritated the hell out of a man or turned him on to the point he couldn't think straight. She had both effects on Cannon.

He had an idea there was a real flesh-and-blood woman behind that tough detective veneer but doubted he'd get a chance to see it. He dropped to the side of the bed and pulled off his boots as he gave that thought more consideration.

Brit in a more intimate setting, dressed in something skimpy and lacy. He imagined tangling his fingers in her shiny hair and gazing into those sky-blue eyes and seeing them glazed with passion.

Enough, cowboy. He yanked off his shirt, then stood and wiggled out of his jeans. He tossed them over a chair and headed for the bathroom.

He was about to step beneath the spray when his cell phone rang. He raced to grab it from his jeans pocket. The ID screen read R.J. Dalton. He resisted the temptation to ignore the call. Like it or not, R.J. Dalton and the Dry Gulch were in his life for the time being.

"Hello."

"How's it going?" R.J. asked. "Did you find out whether or not you're Kimmie's father?"

Cannon explained that the testing would be done the following morning.

"Did you get a chance to talk to Brittany Garner?"

"I did."

"Is she Kimmie's mother?"

"No. Turns out she's Kimmie's aunt." Cannon figured there was no reason to go into details about Sylvie's murder until he knew for certain whether or not Kimmie was his daughter.

"How are things going with the babysitting chores?" Cannon asked.

"Hadley is loving every minute of it. She's like a kid with a new doll. Went shopping today and bought Kimmie a whole wardrobe, like she needs to be gussied up at that age."

"Tell her not to get too attached yet." Or ever, for that matter. Whatever happened, Cannon had no intention of making the Dry Gulch Ranch or R.J. part of his future.

"Baby's right here, kicking like a Rockette in training," R.J. said. "Want to tell her goodnight?"

"No." No way was he coochy-cooing over the phone.

"I'll hold the phone close to her," R.J. said, ignoring his response.

Soft cooing and gurgling sounds reached Cannon's ear. His chest tightened. His stomach grew queasy. The tug on his emotions left his throat so dry he could barely manage a mumbled hello.

"She's smiling," R.J. said. "Must know you're her dad."

"Then she knows more than I do at this point." Cannon said his goodbyes and broke the connection.

Heaven help them all if he was Kimmie's father.

He was toweling off after the shower when he suddenly remembered something Sylvie had said that night they'd been drinking together. He rushed out of the bathroom in the nude, grabbed his jeans and dug Brit's card from the pocket.

He'd punched in all but the last number when he changed his mind. What he remembered wasn't a game changer. It could wait until morning. Give him a good reason to see her again.

And that's when it hit him how much he wanted to see the condescending detective again. Could his life get any more screwed up?

BRIT WAS SLAMMED by the terrible sense of mysterious loss again as she pulled into the garage of her tri-level town house. She'd had a twin sister. They might have shared so many things, a closeness only twins are said to experience. If only they'd met before a killer had claimed Sylvie's life.

Now Brit couldn't help but wonder what other secrets were hiding in her past. Were there other siblings? Had she and Sylvie both been put up for adoption or was it only Brit their biological mother hadn't wanted? Why hadn't her adopted parents ever told her about her twin?

Could she have saved Sylvie from the brutal murder had they met sooner?

Now another question seared into her mind. Why hadn't Sylvie told Cannon that she was pregnant with his child? Now that she'd met Cannon, it was hard to picture him as a man to fear.

Self-confident. Lived on the edge. Might never settle down. A heartache in cowboy clothing. Perhaps not the best of men to hang your heart on, but still he'd deserved to know he was a father.

The mystery continued to plague her thoughts as she killed the engine and climbed out of her silver Acura sedan. Hitting the garage button, the door began its descent as she entered the house though the small laundry-mudroom.

She left her keys on the hook by the back door

and stepped into the kitchen. Anxiety hit like a bolt of lightning. She wasn't alone. Her hand went for her gun as a pair of large, meaty hands grabbed her from behind. He yanked her arms behind her back with so much force she cried out in pain.

He shoved her into the wall, his own large body pushing into hers as he plied her weapon from her fingers. A heavy clunk sounded as it hit the tiled kitchen floor. A heartbeat later the sharp blade of a knife pricked the flesh at the base of her neck.

"A lesson you should have learned from your father. Piss off the wrong people and there will be hell to pay."

Waves of adrenaline combatted the anxiety, revving all her police intuitions and training. Even with the knife at her neck, she struggled to turn enough to see the man's face. His hold was too tight and the knife drew a stream of blood that trickled down her neck.

"How do you know my dad?"

"Wrong question." He laughed and then coughed a raspy rattle that seemed to come from deep in his chest. The blade of the knife slid across her jugular and then down her arm, a promise of the hell to come.

If she did nothing, he was going to kill her.

Brit kicked backward, connecting with the

attacker's right leg hard enough to throw him off balance.

The knife slid to her shoulder, slicing through the flesh painfully as it slashed across her skin, but still he held her arm behind her back so tightly she couldn't move.

"You bitch. Your payback is waiting in the bedroom, all your fault."

He was going to rape and kill her. She bucked the back of her head against him with all the strength she could muster. She heard it crack against his chin.

Unfazed, her assailant pounded his fist into her back and then spun her around to face him. Dizzy from pain, she struggled to focus. All she could make out was a pair of onyx-black eyes glowing like coals.

He hammered her head against the wall with his fist. She sank to the floor, the room a hazy mass of shifting images.

Somehow she spotted the pistol he'd knocked from her hand. She reached for it and her finger found the trigger.

Before she could aim it, his foot connected with her head. Dizzy and disoriented, she aimed into the foggy blur and pulled the trigger.

A filmy black curtain slowly descended on her world.

Chapter Six

Cannon strolled out of the examining room where he'd been swabbed to the nurse's satisfaction. His craving for a cup of strong coffee intensified now that he was allowed to have caffeine.

His muscles were doing some serious protesting of their own, complaining painfully at every move. They'd taken a beating over the past two days, first at the raw power of an angry bull, followed by sitting for hours yesterday behind the wheel of his less-than-luxurious pickup truck.

But he'd done his part. Filled out a multitude of forms and read every word of the documents. He'd also followed the usual list of dos and don'ts from the pre-swabbing directions on the website. He wanted nothing to invalidate or taint the testing. Too much was riding on the result.

Now all that was left to do was the staff and lab director's job of tracking, verifying and performing the statistical calculations. Then he'd know for certain whether or not he was Kimmie's father.

He still couldn't wrap his mind around the full implications of that, but apprehension felt like sandpaper scratching against his nerves.

He ignored the lab exit signs and followed the odor of coffee down a narrow hallway. He stopped at what looked like a staff lounge. Two uniformed police officers were talking between chomping down on chocolate-covered doughnuts.

"Garner's lucky to have come out of that with only minor injuries."

"Still can't believe the intruder got the jump on her." Garner, as in Brit Garner? Cannon's interest zeroed in.

"Is she still in the hospital?" he asked nonchalantly, as if he had a right to be privy to the information.

"Memorial Hermann."

"And the guy who attacked her?"

"Still on the loose last I heard."

Cannon's muscles bunched into frayed knots.

The cops moved on to a different topic. Cannon filled a to-go cup with the strong brew and left. Time to make a hospital call on the gorgeous detective.

"ALL I REMEMBER of his face are his eyes," Brit said for what seemed like the tenth time in as many minutes. She tugged the sheet again, trying to keep the uninjured shoulder that kept escaping the baggy hospital gown from showing.

Her partner, Rick, paced the room. He was hounding her with questions she really wanted to answer, but she'd already explained what she could remember of the attack. Pulling the trigger was the last thing she recalled. Even that memory was vague, as if it had happened to someone else. Were it not for the bandages, the pain in her left shoulder and her killer headache, she could easily believe it had been a nightmare.

"Did the attacker say anything?"

"Not much, or if he did I don't remember it."

"Try. What did he say when he grabbed you?"

"Something about my father."

"What about your father?"

She struggled to remember through the brain fog. "That I should have learned from him. That I piss people off. I can't recall his exact words."

"He must have said more than that. Think, Brit. But don't overdo it," he added, no doubt remembering the nurse's warnings not to upset her.

"I am thinking." She massaged her right temple as if that could coax the words from their hiding place inside her mind. "He was going to drag me to the bedroom."

"I'm sure he was. Son of a bitch," Rick murmured under his breath as he stopped at the foot of her bed.

"Did his voice sound familiar?"

"No, but then nothing much was registering at the time except staying alive."

"Do you remember shooting him?"

"Somehow I managed to get my hands on my weapon when I was sliding into unconsciousness. I think I shot it once. The next thing I knew I was lying on the floor and my neighbor Janie and officers Bates and Cormier were standing over me. I don't know how long I'd been out."

"Only a few minutes. Fortunately, your neighbor heard the gunshot and came running."

"Janie's head of our Neighborhood Watch group. She knows everything that goes on in our neighborhood. Talk to her. She may have seen the guy lurking around the house before he broke in."

"Bates asked. She said she didn't see anything unusual, but I'll talk to her again."

"And no one saw the man leaving my house after the attack?" Brit questioned, just trying to get things straight in her muddled mind.

"No, but he left a trail of blood across your kitchen to the back patio door."

She tried to rise onto her elbows. The dizziness returned. Rick appeared to be swaying.

Rick never swayed. She closed her eyes and let her head fall back to the pillow.

"My blood or his?"

"His, and lots of it. You didn't miss."

"Nice to know he has something to remember me by this morning, as well. Was the lock broken on the patio door?"

"Yeah."

"So much for my alarm system."

"The wires were all cut," Rick said. "He knew what he was doing. He just wasn't counting on you knowing what you were doing."

Satisfaction eased her tension. "Glad I got at least one shot off. Nice to know I can deliver a bullet when I'm passing out."

"A direct hit, too. As much blood as he lost, he should be in a hospital somewhere in the city, but we haven't been able to locate him."

"And you checked with all the emergency rooms?"

"Yep, but we'll find him. We have fingerprints and DNA," Rick said. "If he's in either of those FBI database systems, we should have no trouble getting a positive ID."

Brit tried to push up on her elbows again and this time she made it. She looked around the room. "Where are my clothes?"

"Taken for evidence."

"I can't leave here in this hospital gown."

"Why not? It's your color."

"Not funny."

"That's what Shelly Mince said at the crime scene. She packed a duffel of necessities for you and brought them to the hospital when we finished up at your house last night. You'll want to stay away from there until the place is cleaned up."

"I've seen plenty of blood. Where's the duffel?"

Rick walked over and opened the small closet to the left of her bed. "It's right here. Not that you're going anywhere anytime soon."

"I'm not going to just lie here and stare at the ceiling while the guy who tried to kill me goes on the run and disappears."

"Thanks for that vote of confidence, partner, but you're not the only competent cop in Houston."

"I know that." It didn't change her mind about what she had to do. "What happened to my pistol?"

"We found it at the scene. It's at the precinct."

"At least the rotten bastard didn't steal it."

"On the bright side, he didn't shoot you with it, either."

"Which also makes no sense. Not that I'm complaining. I just need my weapon."

"You don't need one right now," Rick said.

"Captain Bradford ordered round-the-clock protection while you're in the hospital. You have an armed guard at your door now."

"Tell Captain Bradford thanks but she can call off the dogs. Now hand me that duffel so I can get dressed. Then you can drive me to the precinct to get a replacement weapon."

Rick shook his head. "No can do. Doctor's orders."

"I feel fine," she lied.

"That's good to hear."

Brit looked to the door for the source of the last comment. Dr. Simpson, the white-coated young trauma specialist who had taken care of her in E.R. last night stepped inside.

She smiled and eased her head back to the pillow as a new wave of wooziness hit. "Just the man I need to see. I appreciate the wonderful care, but duty calls. If you'll just sign my release papers, I'll give up my bed to the sick and wounded."

"I'm glad to hear you're feeling so well."

"Then you'll sign the release?"

"No."

"Why not?"

"You have a concussion and you lost a good deal of blood from the shoulder wound. You need bed rest and medical observation for at least another twenty-four hours."

"You tell her, Doc." Rick walked over to the bed. "I've got to run, partner. I'll check with you later, but if you remember anything you haven't already told me, call. I'll be out playing cop."

Rick gave his signature wink and double click of his tongue as he escaped, closing the door behind him.

"How's the pain in the shoulder?" the doctor asked.

"I've had worse." She raised her hand and stretched until her fingers crawled across the thick bandage. "When do I get this off?"

"In a few minutes. I'll check the wound and if it looks good, the nurse will apply a new and smaller dressing. How's the headache?"

"Persistent, but the pounding is more like a kid on drums now instead of a jackhammer."

"That's progress. I'll keep you on the current medication. The pounding should disappear entirely soon. How's the vertigo?"

"Much improved."

"Then sounds like you're well on your way to recovery."

"Exactly. So there's really no point in my staying here. I can rest in any bed as easily as I can rest here."

"Yes, but would you? Besides, you're far too unsteady to be left alone."

"I won't be alone. I have a friend I can stay

with and I'll come back to the E.R. immediately if there's a problem."

There was a tap at the door.

"Come in," the doctor said.

He'd probably expected the nurse but it was the guard who stepped inside. "You have a visitor," he said to Brit.

"Who?"

"Cannon Dalton. Do you want me to show him in or turn him away?"

Cannon was the last person she'd expected to see this morning, but there was no reason not to see him except that she no doubt looked like she'd been in a fight with a bulldog. She raked her fingers through her tangled hair and pushed it behind her ears.

"Show him in."

Cannon swaggered in, looking even sexier than he had last night, if that was possible. He was clean-shaven, wearing a pale gold Western shirt that set off his eyes.

He took off his black Stetson and held it in his hands, fingering the brim. A lock of sun-streaked hair fell over his brow.

"Tell me you're not here because there were complications at the lab," she said. "That truly would be the last straw this morning."

"I've been swabbed," he said. "No complications. Doesn't look like you can say the same."

"How did you know I was here?"

"Lab gossip. I figured I'd drop by and see if there's anything I can do to help."

His timing couldn't have been better. Now if he'd just go along with her on this. She smiled appreciatively. "I'm feeling fine," she said, "but Dr. Simpson is concerned about my staying alone."

"If that's an invitation to play nurse, I'm at your service."

She breathed a sigh of relief. "There you have it, Dr. Simpson. I won't be alone."

Cannon smiled, walked over and took her hand as if they were old friends—or more. Heat crept through her veins. She looked away, careful not to let him see that his touch had an effect on her.

"I'll be here for you as long as you need me," Cannon said. "Not sure how good a nurse I am, but I can fetch and carry and I make a mean tortilla soup."

"See, Dr. Simpson," Brit said. "I'll be in great hands."

The doctor didn't look convinced. "You have an armed guard here at the hospital. That indicates to me it wouldn't be safe for you to go back to the scene of the crime or not to have protection."

"I'm a cop," she reminded him. "I made a

mistake and let the man get the jump on me once. I won't be careless enough to do that again. Besides, haven't you heard? He's in far worse shape than I am. I have no idea why they ordered the guard."

"She can stay at my place," Cannon offered.

"Thank you, Cannon. That settles that."

The doctor closed the chart. "I can't keep you here against your will, Detective Garner, but I think you'll be making a serious mistake by going against my recommendations for continued hospitalization."

Certainly not her first. "I'll follow the rest of your instructions to the letter."

"Your decision. I'll check out the shoulder wound and then have the nurse go through the care instructions with both of you," the doctor said. "But I'll need to see you in my office in three days, or before if your condition worsens in any way."

"Not a problem," Brit assured him.

She'd get Cannon to drive her home and then he could do as he pleased until he got the paternity test results. After all, she was a detective. She knew to stay clear of the crime scene; but that left the rest of the town house.

Good thing she didn't really need Cannon to nurse her back to health, though. Scary to think of what kind of TLC you could get from a guy used to tangling with bulls and women he picked up in bars.

No reason to worry. She would be getting nothing but a ride from Cannon Dalton.

CANNON WAS CERTAIN he was being used. He wasn't sure why at this point or even if it was bad thing. On the surface, having the seductive detective so eager to accept his help was enticing. Which meant there was more to this than the obvious.

He held open the passenger door of his pickup truck while Brit climbed inside. Since she'd asked him to step into the hallway while her wound was dressed, this was the first real look he had at the knot on the back of her head and the thickness of the bandage just below her left shoulder blade.

Whoever she'd tangled with had meant business. Cannon couldn't help but wonder if her attack was somehow related to Sylvie's murder. Either way, Brit was lucky to be alive.

She was a cop. She should be able to take care of herself. If not, he was sure the officers on the Houston police force would do their best to defend their own.

Yet, the need to protect her swelled like an obsession inside him. He couldn't explain it. Maybe it was just a man's natural instinct to protect a woman in danger. Maybe it was the emotional roller coaster he'd been on since Kimmie had dropped into his life. Most likely it was a combination of the two.

"Take the first left," Brit said as he pulled out into the traffic lane. "Then watch for the signs for I-20 west."

"That's not the way to my hotel."

"Of course not. It's the way to my town house."

"The crime scene."

"Right. The scene where some rotten bastard tried to kill me. I need to check it out for myself."

"What part of bed rest and not stressing out do you *not* understand?"

"What part of I'm fine do you not understand?"

So that was the game. She had no intention of following any of the doctor's orders. Cannon swerved, made a U-turn and hit the accelerator.

Brit turned so that she was facing him. "What are you doing?" she snapped.

"Taking you back to the hospital. I signed on to make sure you weren't left alone, not to taxi you around town."

"You're kidding, right? I mean you didn't really think I was going to hang out with you in your hotel room?"

"Yeah. Guess I'm not as sophisticated as you.

I usually take a woman at her word when she asks for help."

"I thought you understood and were playing along with me."

"Doesn't really matter what you thought," he said, still prickling. "I'm driving you back to the hospital. After that you're on your own."

"You're as hardheaded as those bulls you ride, Cannon Dalton."

"Don't even try to detail my faults, Detective. You don't know the half of it."

"Look, I'm sorry, Cannon. Let me explain."

"Why bother? I'm just a stupid rodeo cowboy who doesn't get the intricacies of deceit."

She reached across the seat and rested her hand on his arm. "I don't know you well enough to make judgments, but you don't know me that well, either. So give me a break and try to understand where I'm coming from. I risk my life on an almost daily basis to go after killers. It's what I do. The only difference here is that the would-be killer came after me."

"I admire your dedication." He kept driving toward the hospital. "But you're in no shape to go after a jaywalker right now, much less a would-be killer. In my book, trying it is stupidity, not bravery or even duty."

She let go of his arm. "Okay, you win. I'll go to your hotel and rest. But first, just make a quick stop at my house. I need to pick up my computer and some personal items. You surely can't object to that."

He considered the option, knowing she'd probably break her promise the second she got home. But the truth was he wanted to see the crime scene for himself. Not that he had any intention of jumping into the case.

Besides, if he took her back to the hospital, she'd just call a taxi and leave again. At least this way, he'd be there if she had more complications from the concussion.

"On my conditions," he said.

"Your conditions?" Her voice rose. "I'm the one in control…."

He slowed and pulled to the curb. She sputtered like an engine that had run out of fuel. "Okay, let's hear it," she said. "But be reasonable."

"One quick stop at your house, and then on to my hotel. You will rest and stop acting like the safety of the entire town of Houston rests entirely on your shoulders. And stop talking to me like I'm a hired hand."

She rolled her eyes but then managed a half smile. "Deal."

He turned and headed back toward I-20. He decided this was as good a time as any to level with her about the rest of the reason he'd come to the hospital this morning.

"I didn't just come by to check on you this morning."

"Then why did you come?"

"After I left you last night, I remembered something else Sylvie had said when we were in the bar."

She swiveled to face him and zeroed in like a laser. "What is it?"

"I remember Sylvie saying something about time travel. Coming from the past. Going to the past. I may not have heard it right and only remember it because it sounded so crazy to me at the time. And I think she may have mentioned a sister, though I don't remember what she said about her."

Brit turned back to face straight ahead and grew quiet and pensive.

"Are you feeling okay?" he asked after ten minutes of silence."

"Fine. I'm still thinking about the time travel comment. Are you sure she wasn't just talking about her past?"

"I'm not really sure of anything about that night."

Brit understood confusion and not being able to remember details. She was living it right now. But at least her problems stemmed from a concussion, not a whiskey bottle. She told him which exit to take and he nodded in response.

Her head started pounding again. She didn't dare let Cannon know that. He'd turn right around again on a dime.

CANNON HAD A strong hunch that helping Brit escape the hospital had been a huge mistake. On the other hand, he had nothing else to do but sit around and wait for test results, and hanging out with Brit was definitely not boring.

Twenty minutes of heavy traffic later, they pulled up in front of Brit's town house. It was on a cul-de-sac surrounded by other town houses that looked exactly like hers. The streets were deserted, the residents either inside on this glorious fall day or, more likely, at work.

Lawns were meticulously landscaped, separated by thick holly hedges. There were no porches, but each house had impressive brass overhangs to shelter the wide porticos and striking etched-glass-and-mahogany front doors.

The prominent difference was that Brit's front door was striped with police tape.

"I don't suppose you plan to pay any attention to the warning on the tape," Cannon said.

"I don't have to. I'm a homicide detective, remember?"

"How could I forget? I thought they only used that tape when there had been an actual murder."

"Not necessarily. They can use it anytime they don't want the public entering or disturbing an area. Which is why you'll have to wait for me outside."

Brit started up the walk and then veered to the stone walkway that ran between the thick shrubs that separated her house from the one next to it. Maybe she had decided not to cross the tape.

Cannon hurried to catch up with her. Before he could, a black sedan pulled up in front of the house.

A woman appearing to be in her midfifties, short brown hair in a stylish bob jumped out and stamped toward them. "Stop right there," she called in a voice that sounded a lot like Cannon's evil high-school principal.

Brit spun around. "Captain Bradford. What are you doing here?"

"Looking for you. Your doctor said you'd left the hospital against his recommendations. I figured I'd find you here."

"I only plan to take a quick look around and pick up a few personal items. I'll be careful not to disturb a thing, though I suspect the CSU has all the evidence they need by now."

"Going inside is not a good idea in your condition. Go back to the hospital. Give yourself some time. Rick has everything under control here."

"I'm not here to take over and I'm feeling fine," Brit insisted, though she'd looked unsteady walking.

Brit nodded toward Cannon. "My friend did the driving and he's going to stay with me the rest of the day. If there's any problem at all, he can drive me back to the E.R. at once."

The captain frowned, obviously still agitated.

Cannon extended his hand. "I'm Cannon Dalton, rent-a-nurse."

"Cannon Dalton? As in Kimmie Dalton's father?" Bradford turned back to Brit before he could respond to her questions. "Care to explain all of this, Detective Garner?"

"There's nothing to explain. Cannon took the paternity test this morning and then offered to stick around and help out."

"So you've pulled a person of interest in your sister's murder into an attempted murder case involving you?"

"No one mentioned my being a person of interest in a murder case," Cannon protested. His hunch had definitely been right.

"You're only a person of interest because I thought you might have information that could lead to finding Sylvie's killer," Brit insisted.

"Regardless, you are not crossing the police

line," Bradford said. "Brit can go inside, but first we need to have a talk."

"About what?" Brit asked.

"About what I'd hoped not to upset you with until you were feeling better. But since you're here, you leave me no choice."

"Rick's already told me that there's lots of blood."

"That's not the big problem."

"So what is?"

"Your attacker had obviously been in your house for some time before you arrived home," Bradford said. "He did some redecorating of your bedroom using your personal belongings and posters he'd brought with him."

"I've seen extremely grisly crime scenes before. I can handle it," Brit insisted. "But I want to enter through the patio door just as my attacker did. It helps when I'm working a case."

Brit stamped off. Bradford turned back to Cannon. "You may as well come, too. I don't know what it can hurt at this point and I may need you to help me carry her out of here and back to the hospital when the impact of this hits her. It made me nauseous when I saw it and I haven't had a concussion."

"It's that bad?"

"No. It's worse."

Chapter Seven

Brit entered the kitchen and groaned. "I don't know if this will ever come clean. I don't see how he walked away after losing this much blood."

"That's what we all said," Bradford agreed. "Have you seen enough for now?"

"Not until I see what the bastard did to my bedroom."

Bradford followed her as she left the kitchen. Cannon stayed a few steps behind. He hurried to catch up when he heard a gasp followed by a shaky curse.

When he saw what Brit was staring at, he rushed over and put an arm around her to steady her. He wasn't sure if it was fury or revulsion that had her trembling. Both were appropriate.

"That's Sylvie in the pictures," she said. "That's Kimmie's mother."

The images were so sickening that even Cannon's stomach lurched and threatened to revolt.

"What kind of deranged son of a bitch would do something like this?"

"The maniac who killed Sylvie and tried to kill me."

Brit walked over and tore a life-size poster from the wall and ripped it in half. The poster was made from a black-and-white photo of Sylvie lying in an alleyway with her throat slit.

A black lace pantie, apparently Brit's, had been taped to the image. She bit her bottom lip so hard that her teeth left a temporary imprint.

The other poster photos were merely different angles of Sylvie's dead body. Other pieces of Brit's lingerie had been shaped into evocative positions and scattered around the room, either near or attached to the posters.

The bedcovers were pulled back. Cannon shuddered to even think what the assailant's plans had been for this bedroom had he not been shot before he could drag Brit in here.

If he could get hold of the pervert right now, Cannon was sure he could kill him with his bare hands. With any luck, he'd staggered outside and was lying facedown in the mud after a slow death.

"My fault," Brit stammered. "He said this was my fault. He must have been talking about Sylvie's murder. He must have planned to kill both of us as some kind of payback killing."

"But payback for what?" Cannon asked. "You didn't even know about Sylvie until she was murdered. How would he?"

"If we knew that, we'd have our man," Bradford said.

"Where's my weapon?" Brit asked. "I don't have it or my cell phone and I'll need them both."

"CSU turned them and your handbag in," Bradford said. "They're at the precinct. I'll have an officer deliver them to you, once I know where you'll be staying until the doctor tells me you're ready to go back to work."

"I'll be with Cannon."

Relief flooded his body. He wasn't sure when the lines had crossed, but in his mind keeping Brit safe had become his priority, and finding the sick bastard who did this had become his responsibility. He wasn't going anywhere until he was sure this man was dead or behind bars.

Now he only had to convince her of that.

IMAGES FROM THE night before stalked Brit's mind as they escaped the horrid scene and left through the front door of the house. Cannon's hand was at the small of her back, instantly ready to pull her close if she lost her balance.

She well could. The nausea and the headache had returned with a vengeance.

She was haunted by flashes of strong hands jerking and twisting her arm behind her back. The pounding fist. The paralyzing pain as her skull banged against the wall. The deafening crack of gunfire.

But what if the bullet had missed. Then he would have dragged her to the bedroom and waited on her to come to before he raped and killed her. That had undoubtedly been his plan all along.

He wanted her to relive Sylvie's death knowing that she would die the same way. He would have made sure Brit knew who was getting back at her and why. That was what made revenge killings worthwhile.

But who with reason to seek revenge against Brit could have known she had a sister, when Brit hadn't even known it?

"I'm sorry you had to see that," Bradford said.

"I needed to see it," Brit said. "I need to understand the nature of the maniacal pervert I'm dealing with and that he knew more about my biological family than I did. That could be key in identifying him."

"The CSU worked half the night collecting blood samples, shoe prints, fingerprints and any other evidence they considered useful," Bradford said. "It shouldn't take long to get an ID."

"Rick assured me they also checked all the

local emergency rooms for a gunshot victim," Brit said.

"Every hospital within a hundred-and-fifty-mile radius." Brit turned and looked back at the house. "How far was the CSU able to follow the blood trail?"

"To the small man-made creek that runs in back of the town house complex," Bradford said. "Apparently, even with the severe loss of blood, your assailant was still lucid enough to use the water to hide his tracks."

"But he may not have gotten far. Did they search the neighborhood, the bike path through the green area, the park?"

"There's still a team working on that. We'll find who did it," Bradford assured her. "Rick is lead detective on the case, but I've promised him as much manpower as I can spare."

"Rick is capable," Brit agreed, "but I'm the one most affected by this case. Don't you think I should have the lead detective position?"

"Absolutely not. The doctor ordered bed rest. I expect you to follow those orders. I don't want to see you at the precinct for at least a week."

"A week? You can't expect me to do nothing on this case for a week."

"I expect you to follow orders. You've canceled every vacation you've scheduled for the past two years including the one you were supposed to start the morning Sylvie's body was discovered. You're long past due. Get some rest. Read a book. Watch movies. Take a cruise."

"I get seasick."

"Then don't take a cruise, but you're not coming back to work until I clear you. If you decide to stay in Houston, I can provide around-the-clock protection," the captain offered.

"I can protect myself."

The captain tilted her head and stared at Brit as if there was no reason to state the obvious.

"I realize I let the man last night get the jump on me, but it won't happen again. I can live with taking the rest of the day off if you insist, but a week is unthinkable."

"My decision stands. You can resume your investigation into your sister's murder when you come back to work, but the attack on you is Rick's case from here on out. End of discussion."

Brit could see there was no use to argue further. Keep pushing and Bradford might suspend her indefinitely instead of calling her forced noninvolvement a vacation.

But just because she was officially off the case didn't mean she couldn't do some investigating on her own—under the radar.

Now if she could just get rid of this annoying headache and clear the cobwebs from her mind, she could…

"Ready to go?" Bradford asked.

"I'm ready."

In fact, she couldn't wait to get started. Her first order of business would be getting rid of Cannon, although he'd already proved himself to be a lot more responsible and levelheaded than she'd ever expected.

Still, hanging out with her would only pull the hunky cowboy with the easy smile and hypnotic eyes into trouble. Not much chance she'd have to persuade him. He was no doubt already sorry he'd ever offered his help.

But first she would take him up on the offer of his hotel room. The confusion, headache and urgency were taking their toll.

Fatigue made mush of her muscles. The fog refused to lift completely from her brain. Her headache was becoming more intense.

What she needed was a safe place to fall.

Who'd have ever expected that to be Cannon Dalton's hotel room?

THE HACKING COUGH started again, the blood in Clive's throat strangling him. Pain racked his body as he turned his head enough that the blood dribbled from between his lips.

It had been hours, maybe days, since the bullet bit into his stomach, tearing out tissue and muscle and leaving his insides exposed like a butchered calf. He'd lost track of time.

The room was pitch-black, the air dank and fetid with the smell of death. His death, unless help arrived soon.

Where was the dammed doctor? He should have been here by now.

There was a rattling deep in Clive's chest. He struggled to cough, but his throat closed tight. His lungs began to burn.

He heard footsteps. The doctor was coming at last.

Chapter Eight

The hotel room was quiet except for the sounds of Brit's rhythmic breathing. She'd changed out of her jeans for a more comfortable pair of workout shorts and then dropped to the bed and drifted into sleep within minutes after they'd arrived at the hotel.

Thankfully, Cannon had splurged for a nicer hotel than usual. He'd figured he'd only be in town a night or two at the most and he was too sore to risk a bed that wouldn't be kind to his strained and bruised muscles.

Cannon took out his small laptop, turned it on and waited for the slow start-up on his aging machine. About the only thing he used it for was checking out rodeo schedules and results.

Until he'd learned he might be a father, his life had been simple and uncomplicated. Chasing the dream from one rodeo to another. Hoping to avoid injury so that he could pick up enough points to be in serious contention for the big bucks and the national title.

So far, no national title, but he couldn't complain. He'd earned over $300,000 in prize money last year along with countless buckles and his new pickup truck. Most of the more expensive buckles he'd won were tucked away in a safe-deposit box in Austin. The cash was invested or residing in his savings account in the same bank.

Another good year and he might just start looking for the ranch he planned to settle on when he had enough money saved to stock it.

When that day came, he'd figured he might even find a woman to share the dream. Start a family. Settle down. In the meantime, he was careful to have no surprise packages like Kimmie to shatter the big picture.

One night that he could barely remember may have destroyed it beyond repair. He couldn't drag a baby from rodeo to rodeo. And he wasn't about to dump Kimmie at the Dry Gulch Ranch the way he'd been dumped at his uncle's ranch.

Never wanted. Never liked.

Cannon typed Sylvie Hamm into the search engine and waited to see what it coughed up. He checked out the possibilities. None appeared to match with the Sylvie Hamm who had given birth to Kimmie.

He tried the online social connections and

didn't find her there, either. Not a major shock to him. He wasn't on any of the other popular websites for touching base with people he didn't care about, anyway.

He clicked on the newspaper article that had apparently appeared in the *Houston Chronicle* the day after Sylvie's death. It covered only spotty details about her murder, nothing as graphic as the enlarged photos taped to Brit's walls. Photos taken by the killer himself, most likely shot with the intention of showing them to Brit before he killed her.

The article did state that her body had been discovered in a back alley. He recognized the name of the cross streets. He and Brit had passed them last night on the way to Jodie's Grill. The estimated time of death indicated she'd been killed in broad daylight. Her handbag and all of her identifications were missing.

So Sylvie had been murdered in the vicinity of Brit's office. He wondered if she lived or worked in the area herself. Or was it possible that she been on her way to see Brit?

Could she have come that close to connecting with her twin sister after all these years only to be killed before they actually met?

Cannon turned to stare at Brit and a crazy kick of awareness rocked his soul. There was no explaining the way the lady detective got to him. He'd always run from complications before. No one came with more complications than Brit and they were multiplying by the minute.

Last night's assailant wasn't just using scare tactics. He'd murdered Sylvie as payback to Brit. There was no reason to doubt that as soon as he was physically able he'd be back to finish off Brit.

The smartest thing Brit could do right now was accept her boss's offer of 24/7 protection— or else get out of Houston and find a safe place to get some R & R. Come to think of it, getting out of Houston was an excellent idea.

She had a week off. She could go anywhere.

Unfortunately, he had a rodeo looming in a few days if his muscles healed enough to give him a fighting chance with the bull.

There was a tap at the door to the hotel room. Cannon jumped to his feet and hurried over before the noise woke Brit. He looked out the peephole. Captain Carla Bradford was standing there with two handbags slung across her shoulder.

Cannon opened the door, checked to make sure his key was in his pocket and then stepped into the hallway, closing the door behind him.

"Brit's sleeping," he explained. "I hate to wake her unless this is an emergency."

"No, I just stopped by to give her this." She

handed him a black, leather handbag. "Her pistol is inside the zipped pocket. Be careful with it."

"I can handle a gun," Cannon assured her. Fact was, he was licensed to carry and had a pistol in his truck. "I thought Brit said you were sending an officer by with that."

"I was coming this way."

He doubted that was the full story. The captain was too far up the totem pole to be running errands in Houston traffic.

"Is there anything new in the investigation?" he asked.

"Nothing of consequence."

"You mean nothing you can tell me?"

"Nothing personal, Mr. Dalton. This is an active investigation and you are not an officer of the law."

"I'm an outsider. Got it. I'll let Brit know you made a personal delivery of her possessions."

"How is she?"

"She fell asleep right after we got to the hotel and hasn't woken since."

"Good. She needs to rest, although I'm surprised it's in your hotel room, considering the two of you only met for the first time last night. That was when you met, isn't it?"

"It is. I'm loyal and trustworthy, Captain Bradford. And as lovable as a teddy bear—

unless someone gives me reason to get tough. Brit is safe with me."

"It's not you I'm worried about, Mr. Dalton. It's a man who's on a death mission with her as the target. But since I'm here, I'd like to see for myself that she's actually still with you and not out chasing her killer on her own."

"I thought you might." Cannon took the hotel key from his pocket and pushed it into the lock. At the click he opened the door enough for the captain to peek inside.

Brit had rolled over but was still sleeping, her shiny hair haloing the white pillow. The sheet curled around her, hitting just below her T-shirt clad breasts.

"Satisfied?" he whispered.

She nodded as he closed the door. "I don't know how you got her to rest, but if you have any ideas about being a hero and saving her, forget it. You have no idea what you're up against."

"I'm just the chauffeur. I have no intention of playing cop."

"Then we agree on something. Remind Brit I expect her to keep me posted if she leaves town—which I still think is the best decision at this time. Her would-be killer lost too much blood to go chasing her around the country in the next few days."

"I'll give her the message."

By the time Cannon reentered the room, Brit was curled into the fetal position on the far side of the king-size bed, leaving most of the mattress free.

Cannon took off his boots and stretched out on the bed beside her, fully clothed, on top of the covers. His mind wrestled with the situation.

Brit had given in to a nap, but he knew this wouldn't last. As soon as she felt steady on her feet she'd jump right back into the investigation—with or without Bradford's permission. Worse to do it under the radar. That left her without other officers to watch her back.

He agreed that the best decision would be for her to leave the Houston area. Somehow he didn't see that happening—not unless the investigation led her somewhere else.

Nor did he see her spending another day hanging out with him. Or ever seeing him again if she found out he wasn't the biological father of her niece.

Cannon didn't realize he'd fallen asleep until he woke with a burning deep inside his gut. Brit had obviously tossed in her sleep and ended up cuddled against him. One of her arms stretched across his chest. Her bare left leg pushed between his thighs. Her disheveled hair brushed his chin.

Raw, visceral need bucked around inside him.

His body grew rock-hard, his erection pushing hard against the zipper of his jeans. The craving to pull her into his arms and find her lips with his raged inside him.

For a second he couldn't breathe. Couldn't swallow. Couldn't produce a rational thought.

Finally he managed a few deep breaths and the good sense to ease himself from beneath her arm and off the bed.

But the damage had been done. There was no denying his infatuation for her now, no pretending that the attraction wasn't growing out of control.

Any way you cut it, Cannon was in for trouble.

BRIT OPENED HER eyes and stretched, confused for a minute about where she was or why. Slowly the details fitted themselves together. The attack. The concussion. The nightmarish posters. Cannon.

She glanced around the room. He was bent over a computer, his focus glued to whatever he was reading. He was shirtless, shoeless, his hair slightly rumpled. The awareness he ignited hit again, sending her senses reeling.

Had someone told her twenty-four hours ago she'd experience these sensual jolts, much less trust Cannon enough to move into his hotel room, she'd have thought them nuts.

The only explanation was the timing. She couldn't remember having ever felt this vulnerable. It wasn't that she'd learned anything new from the sickening photos, but they'd been upsetting all the same. So was finding out that she might be the reason Sylvie had been murdered.

Still, Brit could have made it on her own. Having Cannon around had made it a lot easier. Even now, she didn't trust herself to drive, and she wasn't about to sit around and twiddle her thumbs for a week, no matter what Carla Bradford had ordered.

She sat up in bed. There was no reoccurrence of the vertigo that had plagued her this morning. The headache was almost gone, as well. Only the dull, thudding pain in her shoulder remained, triggered by her every move. She stretched and slid out from under the covers.

Cannon turned in his chair. His lips split into a slightly crooked smile that deepened the dimple in his chin. "The sleeping beauty awakes."

"Working on it." She was pretty sure the word *beauty* had been applied loosely. Impulsively, she raked her fingers through her hair, tucking the wild mussed locks behind her ears. Then she straightened the T-shirt that had bunched around her waist.

"How do you feel?" Cannon asked.

"Better," she said, thankful it was the truth.

"At least physically. Emotionally, I'm vacillating between fury that I let the lunatic escape last night and frustration that Bradford's ordered me out of the loop."

"From the amount of blood that covered your kitchen floor, I'm not sure the guy is still alive."

"Apparently he was alive enough to get out of the neighborhood."

"He could have had an accomplice nearby driving the getaway car."

"The possibility of having two lunatics out there looking to kill me doesn't make me feel the least bit better."

She glanced at the bedside clock. Ten minutes after five o'clock. Obviously not correct. "What time is it?"

"Ten after five."

"No way. I couldn't have slept that long."

"Yep, you were out of it."

"Why didn't you wake me?"

"Now why would I do that when the doctor said you needed rest and your boss said you were on vacation?"

She slung her feet over the side of the bed. "I wasted a day."

"Worse, you missed lunch," Cannon said.

"I need a shower more than food." She'd never felt dirtier in her life. It was as if the filthy perversion in her bedroom had crept into every cell of her body. "And I'll need to change into something besides these workout shorts and T-shirt to go out."

"How about room service?" Cannon asked. "I checked out the dinner menu offerings. They look pretty good, and you won't have to bother with changing."

"Fine by me." Bread and water would be fine by her this evening.

Cannon picked up a menu and tossed it to the side of the bed next to her. "Everything from bratwurst to filet mignon."

"I'd best stick to something light until I'm sure the nausea isn't just taking a break."

"But you're not dizzy or nauseous now?"

"Not at the moment. Not even a headache."

"It's the nursing," he said. "I'm extremely experienced in dealing with contusions and concussions, usually my own. Fortunately, I haven't had a concussion since I mastered the art of getting bucked off a bit more gracefully."

"Obviously a man of many talents."

"Yep. See how lucky you are to have me around."

"Let's see, since you've arrived in town I've been attacked and nearly killed. I've had deranged pictures of my sister's murder plastered around the walls of my bedroom. And I've been ordered to take an unwanted vacation. You have a strange definition of lucky."

"But without me riding to your rescue, you could be in the hospital tonight, dressed in that baggy, open-backed gown and about to dine on broth and gelatin."

"There is that." She studied the menu offerings. "I think I'll go with the club sandwich and a cup of tomato soup."

"What do you want to drink?"

"I'll stick with water with lemon."

"How about dessert?"

"None for me. In fact, I can halve the sandwich with you if you want. I'll never eat it all."

"Half a sandwich wouldn't get me past the appetizer stage. I'm thinking a bowl of Texas chili for starters. Followed by the rib-eye steak with fries and a hunk of their fresh-baked bread."

"All washed down with a cold beer," she added for him.

"How'd you guess?"

She shook her head in wonder. "How do you keep from getting to be the size of those bulls you ride?"

"I'm a growing boy."

That wasn't far from the truth. "How old are you?"

"Twenty-seven."

Three years younger than she was. He could

have passed for his early twenties. In spite of his appetite, he was in great shape. Lean and hard-bodied. She supposed he'd have to be strong and agile to stay on a bucking bull.

Brit looked around the room for her purse but didn't spot it. "Did an officer drop off my hand-bag and Smith & Wesson?"

"No, but Captain Bradford did. I think she wanted to assure herself that I hadn't taken you captive. I get the feeling she doesn't like me much."

"Welcome to the club. So where's my weapon?"

"In the closet, inside your handbag."

Cannon made the call to room service. Brit retrieved her phone from her handbag. No calls. She'd hoped for news of suspects from Rick. She checked the pistol and made sure it was easily accessible, loaded and with the safety on. She dropped her phone into her pocket.

Once in the bathroom, she spent agonizing minutes staring into the mirror. Dark circles cupped her eyes. Lines from the pillow creased the skin on her cheeks. Her hair was a dishev-eled mop.

One thing for sure, Cannon Dalton wasn't hanging around because he was enamored of her looks. Not that she wanted him to be.

She turned on the faucet, dipped her hands under the spray and splashed the cool water onto her face. She brushed her teeth again. The metallic taste lingered, probably from the drugs. She'd taken two pills before she lay down.

Her mind went back to the problems at hand. She tried to arrange the events of the past twenty-four hours into a rational pattern, but it was like trying to work a children's pegboard, where all the holes were round and all the pegs were square.

The only thing she was sure of was that the attack was an act of revenge and the would-be killer hadn't started with her. For all she knew, he might not be planning on ending with her, either.

He might have a history of convictions and be going after everyone who'd ever arrested him and their families, as well.

That didn't seem nearly as far-fetched when she remembered the killer's comment about her father. Not that she suspected he'd killed her father. Very unlikely that he'd have waited three years to kill again.

Unless he'd been incarcerated between then and now.

After his years in the police business and coming up through the ranks to land the position of chief of police, the number of people who held a grudge against her father was legend.

She took a long shower and then slipped

into a pair of worn and comfortable jeans and a sweatshirt.

When she rejoined Cannon in the bedroom, he'd pulled two chairs up to a round table. She took one of them. He took the other. "Feel like talking?" he asked.

"I assume you don't mean about the weather."

"Not much we can do about the weather, though the first cold front of the season is headed our way. Should feel like winter by the weekend."

"That covers the weather. If you have questions about the attack, I'm fresh out of answers."

"I have confidence that you'll get on top of the situation once you're back on the job." He leaned back in his chair and crossed his arms over his broad chest. "I ran a computer search on Sylvie Hamm while you were sleeping."

Clearly Cannon's focus was still on the reason he'd come to Houston in the first place. He was here to find out if he had a daughter. Naturally he'd be curious about Kimmie's mother.

Once he got the results of the paternity test, his work would be done in Houston. There would be no reason for him not to bail on Brit and her problems. She needed to keep that straight in her own mind.

"I'm not sure what you learned about Sylvie

on the internet, but I told you most of what I know about her last night."

"Then I must have missed a few of the finer points. How is it you didn't realize you had a twin sister before now? Wouldn't your birth certificate indicate that?"

"I was adopted as an infant so I have an adoption decree not a birth certificate."

"You're a cop. Can't you get a copy of the original?"

"Possibly. I'll try in time, but up until now that hadn't been pertinent to the murder investigation. Finding and arresting her killer was far more pressing than figuring out our birth history."

"Does that mean you haven't identified your and Sylvie's biological mother?"

"I know who our mother was, but she died a few years ago from cancer. I haven't identified our biological father as yet, but Sylvie's stepfather is working in Guam and so far I haven't been able to reach him."

"Was Sylvie also put up for adoption at birth?"

"Her birth certificate didn't indicate that. I did find a copy of her birth certificate in a file with other important papers inside her home."

"Then you should have the name of your birth father."

"None was listed. I assume our birth mother

wasn't married. That may explain why we were separated at birth. She might have felt she could only afford to raise one child, or health issues may have made her only feel capable of raising one child. She chose Sylvie."

"Are there other family members?"

"Sylvie has one younger half brother, which makes him my half brother, too, though neither of us knew the other existed."

"Have you been in touch with him?"

"By phone. Briefly."

"Where is he now?"

"I'm not sure. He's a Navy Seal, currently on a secret mission. He said he hasn't even talked to Sylvie in over a year. They kind of lost touch after their mother died. He said his mother had never mentioned Sylvie being a twin and had never mentioned giving up any child for adoption."

"Interesting."

"Yes, though that means he's been zero help in the investigation. But he did have a lot of questions about Kimmie. I think it's likely he'll get in touch with you when he finishes his mission."

"*If* it turns out that Kimmie is my daughter."

"Right." Even without the test results, Brit was almost certain that she was.

"I read online the little the *Houston Chronicle* had to say about Sylvie's murder," Cannon said.

"It covered the basics, which was all we had at the time, not that we have much more now," Brit admitted.

"It gave the address where she was dragged into an alley and stabbed to death. Not too far from your office in police headquarters. Did she live or work in that area?"

"Oddly no. She lived in Katy and worked at home as a medical transcriptionist."

"What was she doing in the city that morning?"

"All I know is that she took a bus into town and got off a few blocks from where she was stabbed to death. We have security photos from nearby buildings that show her getting off the bus and crossing the street. We lost her after that."

"So there was a chance she was coming to see you that morning."

It hadn't taken him long to figure that out.

"That is one of the possibilities we were looking into. I'm not at liberty to tell you more," she said. Not that she knew much more. The clues had dried up like a raisin in the sun—until the posters in Brit's bedroom had linked Sylvie's death with Brit.

She really needed to talk to Rick. He should

have something to go on by now. So why hadn't he called? Surely he didn't really believe she intended to follow the captain's orders to stay completely out of this.

"Excuse me," she said, "but I have to make a phone call that can't wait."

She picked up her phone and took it to the bathroom. Better not to drag Cannon into this for his own safety. She had to reestablish the boundaries. No matter how easy he was to talk to, they were not a team.

Rick's number was on speed dial. In seconds, his mobile number was ringing.

"I figured you'd be calling soon," he said as a greeting. "Knew it was only a matter of time before you balked at your forced vacation."

"Glad we have that clear. Why didn't you tell me about the blown-up photos of Sylvie's murdered body when we talked this morning?"

"Because I knew you'd jump out of bed and leave the hospital, which I've heard that you did, anyway."

"Now that I know revenge against me and Sylvie's murder are linked, I have a lot better chance of figuring out who killed Sylvie."

"Really? Let's hear what you've come up with."

"Nothing yet," she admitted reluctantly.

"And I don't see how you will until you learn a lot more about Sylvie than you currently know."

"So what do you suggest?"

"Going with what we know. Figure out who has a serious grudge against you and the opportunity to come after you."

"What have you got?"

"Unfortunately, not a lot," Rick said. "I've spent most of the day checking out every criminal who falls within those parameters."

"Any luck?"

"You've helped send a lot of guys to jail since making homicide detective. You have enemies out the kazoo."

"Name me a good cop who doesn't."

"Good point."

"Who tops the list?" Brit asked.

"There are three suspects sharing top spot. Two male. One female."

"Let's hear them."

"Gary Palmer. You remember him, killed his wife and her lover three years ago."

"One of my first cases after making homicide detective. How could I forget?"

Gary Palmer was running for city councilman at the time, though most thought he had little chance of winning. He'd always sworn his innocence, falsely claimed that Brit had tampered with the evidence. The jury had decided with the prosecution. The evidence against him had been too compelling.

"I remember the trial and the sentence," Brit answered. "He got life without parole."

"And last year he got a new sly, sleazy lawyer who's persuaded a judge he should be retried due to our handling of the evidence."

"That case was handled by the book. I made sure of it."

"Nonetheless, he's out on bail while his attorney prepares for a new trial."

"If he's getting a new trial, it seems stupid for him to risk another murder charge. Not that I don't want him checked out, but who else do you have?"

"Hagan Daugherty, better known as the butcher."

"Who could forget good old Hagan?"

Carved up his girlfriend's furniture and her face before plunging the butcher knife into her heart. He'd become romantically fixated on Brit during the investigation and sent her creepy love letters from prison. No one had ever freaked her out more.

"He was placed in an out-of-state psychiatric facility for treatment," she said. "Surely he wasn't released early."

"Afraid so, considered mentally capable of returning to the public two months ago."

He was a definite possibility. She wouldn't put anything past him. "Where is Hagan now?"

"No one seems to know. I've got a team tracking him down. I'll let you know as soon as we get anything on him."

"Which leaves suspect three," Brit said.

"Melanie Crouch."

"The Melanie Crouch who paid someone to kill her rich plastic surgeon husband?"

"That's the one."

Melanie was a piece of work. Attractive. Could pull tears from thin air. Had the jury and the judge in the palm of her hands.

"Melanie did her time and was released last month, a little early, for good behavior," Rick said.

"Yeah. She was a sweetheart. Let's see, how many threatening letters did she manage to get mailed to me from her prison cell?"

"I'd say at least a half dozen that first year. They slowed down after that, but that doesn't mean she didn't keep harboring her grudge."

"Where is she now?"

"According to probation records her official residence is an old farmhouse that once belonged to her grandparents and hasn't been lived in for years. Apparently she inherited it."

"Where is this house?"

"It's near the small town of Oak Grove.

Which, if I remember correctly, is also where you dropped off your niece, Kimmie, last week."

"It is, but I can't see Melanie living in an old run-down house."

"My guess is she won't be there long," Rick said. "Or else she can't afford to live anywhere else. Having your husband killed disqualifies a wife from collecting on his insurance and estate."

"I'd be willing to bet she has some cash stashed away," Brit said. "She went to too much trouble to plan the *almost* perfect murder to risk losing everything."

"Yes, but she'd planned to have all his money and would have if you hadn't seen through her grieving-widow act. But, then, it wasn't a woman who attacked you last night."

"No, but she has a record of paying someone else to do her dirty work."

"The assassin she hired to take out her late husband is still in prison. Not that she couldn't hire someone new."

"I'd like to question her as a person of inter-est. It would also give me a chance to check on Kimmie."

"Fine by me," Rick quipped. "All you have to do is clear it with Bradford and the sheriff of the county where she's residing now."

Bradford wouldn't be easy, but surely the captain would come around after she realized Brit was fine. Besides, they were always shorthanded in Homicide. This would keep Rick or one of the other detectives from having to make the drive up to Oak Grove.

"I've got a call in to the sheriff now," Rick said. "Waiting on him to call me back, but there shouldn't be a problem there. His name is Walter Garcia. He's been sheriff there for quite a while."

Brit's mind jumped ahead. She was on vacation. No reason she had to clear this with Bradford before she made the trip to Oak Grove. It would save time when she got the okay.

Brit's father had always said a good cop did what it took to get the job done.

Brit was a very good cop.

Chapter Nine

Cannon had been suckered. No doubt about it. Following along with Brit's bizarre plans like some tail-wagging puppy. As a result he was driving north on I-45, a few miles over the speed limit, heading to the one spot in Texas he dreaded visiting.

He hadn't bought for a second the idea that she'd decided to follow her boss's order and take a short vacation, out of town, away from the investigation and danger. The shift in plans had come too swiftly and suspiciously immediately after her phone conversation with her partner.

She had something up her sleeve, possibly dangerous and definitely connected to the investigation. But then, he had time to kill while he waited on the test results. Might as well play bodyguard-accomplice to the gorgeous detective instead of just sitting around an expensive hotel in the heart of Houston.

He'd never been one for big-city life. Too

much traffic, too many people, no wide-open spaces. But still, he could have done without the Dry Gulch Ranch.

A few days bonding with her niece while she took care of whatever it was that she was planning to do in the Dallas area was all well and good for Brit.

Bonding with a helpless infant who already held some kind of mesmerizing power over him was the last thing Cannon needed. There would be plenty of time for that if he found out she actually was his daughter. Until then, he could do without poopy diapers and bottle feedings and tiny fingers that curled around his.

And he damn sure didn't need R.J. Dalton. Those days were long gone.

Yet here he was, heading to the Dry Gulch Ranch. Sucker.

Cannon stopped for gas at the Conroe exit. He poked his head back into the car after the tank was filled. "You need anything? Coffee? A soft drink."

"A bottle of water would be nice."

"You got it."

He got his own strong black coffee from the self-serve bar in the convenience store and picked up a bottle of water for her.

When he returned to the car, she was studying

a map of Texas she'd pulled from the door pocket of his truck.

"I know the way to the Dry Gulch," he said.

"I was just checking the distance." She folded the map and put it away.

Cannon turned the key in the ignition and drove away from the pumps and toward the interstate entrance ramp.

"Don't you think we should call your father and make sure he's okay with our staying there a few days?

The word *father* kicked up a surge of ire. "Let's get a couple of things straight before we go any farther, Brit. Number one, R.J.'s never been father to me and I have no intention of participating in a happy family charade now. Second, I don't intend to stay at the ranch long. As soon as I get the results of the paternity test, no matter how it comes out, I'm gone."

"What about Kimmie?"

Good question. He hadn't fully faced that yet. But he'd figure it out without the help of R.J. Dalton.

"If I'm her father, I'll find a way to take care of her," he stated, trying to sound a lot more confident than he felt. The truth was, he had no idea what he'd do with Kimmie.

"You have a great support system in R.J. and the rest of your family," Brit said. "If you moved onto the Dry Gulch, I'm sure they'd be a big help in taking care of Kimmie."

"Right. You had me investigated, which means you have to know my lifestyle isn't baby-friendly. I'm surprised you decided to contact me at all since you seem to think rodeo cowboys are an irresponsible lot."

"Sylvie left specific instructions that if something happened to her, you should be given custody of Kimmie. I couldn't very well ignore her wishes. And, by law, you are the next of kin."

"So why drop her off at the Dry Gulch instead of with me?"

"Leave her at a rodeo with wild bulls snorting all around her?"

"Have you ever even been to a rodeo?"

"No. Let's keep it that way."

Not if he could help it. Detective Brit Garner needed a new taste of Texas.

"I don't know what your past is with R.J.," Brit said. "But it would be nice for Kimmie to have a grandfather and uncles, aunts and cousins in her life."

"Apparently your research didn't give you the full story," he said. "Kimmie isn't going to grow up with a grandfather no matter where I live. R.J. has an inoperable brain tumor. His days are numbered, though the tumor hasn't progressed as rapidly as he'd indicated when he invited all his sons and one daughter to the reading of his will."

"He's already had the reading of the will?"

"He's an unconventional man, when it suits his purpose."

"Which was?"

"To prove what a good father he'd have been if he'd been sober or healthy or had given a damn about anyone but himself. Pardon my French."

"I work in the police department, Cannon. I'm used to far worse language than that. So what did the will say that you find so offensive?"

Cannon hadn't planned to get into this with Brit. He couldn't see why she'd even care. But if she was going to spend her days at the ranch for whatever purpose, she'd probably hear some version of the will's stipulations, anyway.

"In order to share in the estate, each sibling is required to spend one full year living on the ranch and assisting in its operations."

"What if R.J. hadn't lived for a year?"

"The will won't be fully executed until the second anniversary of his death. As long as you take up residence before his death, you can make the cut to start your year."

"I can see why some of the people affected might find that kind of manipulation of their careers and lifestyles problematic. But you're a rodeo cowboy. Living at the ranch between rodeos should fit you perfectly."

"Having any part of my life dictated by R.J. Dalton is problematic to me. Besides, I have plans to buy my own ranch and run it my way. Having six people running a ranch will be chaos."

"Maybe," Brit said. "Maybe not. It would all depend on the people."

"I have no intention of finding out."

"What's the payoff if you meet the will's requirements?"

"The estate is said to be worth around eight million dollars. That includes land, house, outbuildings and cash and investments."

"I didn't realize there was that much money to be made in ranching," Brit said.

"There seldom is unless your cows are scratching their backs on oil wells. R.J's aren't, though his neighbors the Lamberts are one of the richest families in Texas."

"If the Dry Gulch is worth eight million, it must be reasonably successful."

"Didn't look that way to me when I was there for the reading of the will. The house was run-down. I didn't see a lot of livestock when I took the tour of the ranch that R.J. provided. Have to admit R.J. did have an impressive group of horses, though."

"He must have gotten the money somewhere. Why did your parents split?"

That, Cannon was not discussing with the gorgeous detective. "Mother had her reasons for leaving. Now I'd best make that call to R.J. so the old coot doesn't meet us at the door with a shotgun. Unless you've changed your mind about staying at the ranch."

"Then what? We'd sleep in the truck."

"I have before. I don't recommend it. There's a small motel in Oak Grove. We could stay there and it would still be convenient for visiting with Kimmie—if that's your only business in Oak Grove."

"No, thanks. I'm intrigued more than ever at the prospect of getting to know Kimmie's grandfather."

That figured. He used the hands-free function in his new truck to make the call. The phone rang so many times he was about to hang up when he heard R.J.'s throaty hello.

"This is Cannon."

"Yep. Recognized your voice. You got those test results back already?"

"Not yet."

"I'll be jiggered. What's taking 'em so long? You'd think they were having to make the DNA, not just figure it out."

"I hope to hear tomorrow, or the next day for sure."

"I'd hope so. Guess you're calling to check on Kimmie. She just left to go home with Leif and Joni for the night. No shortage of babysitters around here. They've all taken to her like a hog to persimmons."

"Glad to hear she's being well cared for." As for the Dalton clan taking to her, Cannon wasn't sure that was for the best. He didn't need them putting pressure on him to bring her to the Dry Gulch for visits.

"I know it's late to be calling you about this," Cannon said, "but I was hoping you were in the mood for company."

"You're not company. You're family. Always got a bed for you."

"I'm not coming by myself."

"No problem there, either. You wouldn't by any chance be bringing Kimmie's mama home with you, now would you?"

"No. Do you remember the police detective who dropped Kimmie off at the ranch?"

"That's the woman I'm talking about."

"Turns out she's not Kimmie's mom. She's actually her aunt."

"Hell's bells. Go figure that. Where's the mama?"

"She was murdered last week."

A period of silence followed. Cannon waited for R.J. to get his mind around that bombshell.

"I'm real sorry to hear that," R.J. said. "They arrest somebody for the crime?"

The conversation was drifting in the wrong direction. "Not yet. We can discuss that later. The reason I'm calling is that Detective Garner has a few days off work and she would like to spend it on the ranch, getting to know Kimmie a little better, if that's okay with you."

"Really? The detective wants to come here? She couldn't get away fast enough when she dropped Kimmie off."

"You'll have to ask her about that."

"Kind of surprising that a Houston homicide detective would be vacationing when her sister's killer hasn't been arrested."

The old man might have a brain tumor but he was astute enough to read between the lines. "Brit will explain about that later," Cannon said. R.J. would probably buy the story that she was just following orders after suffering a concussion.

Cannon wasn't. There was more to the sudden decision to drive to Dry Gulch tonight than just bonding with Kimmie, especially after the past twenty-four hours she'd had.

"Are you coming with the detective?" R.J. asked.

"I'm driving her to the ranch. I'll only be staying until I get the test results."

"So you two are driving up here in the morning?"

"Actually we're on our way there now. Should make it to Oak Grove about ten and to the Dry Gulch shortly after that."

Brit grabbed his arm. "Eleven," she whispered. "Tell him we'll be there around eleven."

The plot thickened. No surprise. Detective Brit definitely had an ulterior motive. "Make that eleven," Cannon said.

"Okeydokey. I'll probably be in bed by then, but there's leftovers and half a pecan pie in the fridge, made with pecans from right here on the Dry Gulch. Help yourself to that or anything else you see that you want."

"We've eaten."

"A cowboy's stomach can always make room for pie. There's a guest room down the hall and several more upstairs."

"Where will we find a key?"

"No one bothers with keys out here. I'll leave the door unlocked. Usually do, anyway. Armadillos and coyotes can't work the doorknobs yet and don't no troublesome strangers wander this far off the road. At least not since we took care of the troublemaking hombre who made Faith and Cornell's life a living hell."

"Who's Faith and Cornell?"

"Faith's your half brother Travis's wife. Cornell is her son. Talk about a young man taking to the cowboy life. Hard to get him off a horse. Bet he's ridden almost every inch of the Dry Gulch."

Cannon finished the conversation quickly, not about to feign interest in a bunch of people he wouldn't be around long enough to get to know.

Brit was so quiet for the next few minutes he thought she might have dozed off. He upped his speed. She opened her eyes, looked at him and frowned.

"I can arrest you for going more than the speed limit, you know."

"If you were a stickler for the rules, you wouldn't be heading to Oak Grove."

"I'm just taking a vacation as my supervisor ordered."

"Is that so? Then I guess we're going to be making out between the hours of ten and eleven."

"Dream on, cowboy."

"So what are we going to be doing with our time or is that so confidential that if you tell me you have to kill me?"

"Not quite, but the less you know about this investigation, the better off you'll be. So I've been thinking, and I have a proposition for you."

"Unless it's in the same ballpark as making out, the answer is probably no."

"Hear me out. I'm feeling much better now and the vertigo seems to have run its course. So I could just drop you off at the ranch and then borrow your truck for a bit."

"Sorry, my truck doesn't go anywhere without me."

"Then don't say I didn't warn you."

"WHAT IN THE Sam Hill is going on now?" R.J. muttered under his breath as he rambled to the front of the house. He'd figured the detective was mad as a wet hen at Cannon when she'd dropped Kimmie off at the ranch. Now here she was driving to the ranch with him to visit her niece.

Sure hadn't taken Cannon long to cool her down. Must have inherited some of R.J.'s charm where women were concerned. Hopefully he was better at holding on to them than R.J. had been.

R.J. pushed open the screen door and stepped onto the wide porch. The night was filled with the songs of tree frogs and crickets and the call of a hoot owl on a low branch of a lonesome pine. The heaven was a showcase of twinkling stars. A cool breeze tossed around his thinning, gray hair.

Winter was tiptoeing in on them, but there hadn't been a frost yet and it would be Christmas in another couple of weeks. R.J. had never expected to live to see another Christmas, but God was smiling down on him sure as shooting. Not that he deserved it.

He'd pretty much wasted what might have been a blessed life. Didn't even remember half of it. Lost reality to booze. Lost his money to gambling. Chased too many women that weren't worth catching while losing the women who were.

He'd been to the post and tied the knot four times and never made one of his wives happy enough that they'd stuck it out to the finish line. Not that he blamed them. He had more demons on his back than most dogs had fleas.

Best he could say for himself was that he'd never killed a man, though he'd met a few that he wanted to. Never got a woman pregnant he didn't marry, except for Kiki. She stayed around long enough to give birth to their daughter, Jade, and then she'd taken off for Hollywood.

Never heard from her again. Hadn't heard from Jade, either, until the reading of the will, and she hadn't bothered to call or stop by since. He hadn't really expected to hear from her, but, then, he'd all but given up on hearing from Cannon again, too.

Never knew when the odds would change. Something about Cannon made R.J. think they'd really hit it off if they could move past the old resentments.

R.J. would be sittin' in high cotton if Cannon did settle down on the Dry Gulch, at least when he wasn't riding the circuit. Might even marry Brit Garner. He could do a damn sight worse. She was pretty as a pasture full of wildflowers. And Kimmie could grow up right here on the Dry Gulch Ranch.

Two detectives in the Dalton family.

His old drinking and gambling buddies would get a horse laugh out of that.

Not that there was any guarantee Cannon would hang around long. Still, sure be good if he did.

R.J. owed it all to his beautiful neighbor Caroline Lambert. She was the one who'd encouraged him to get in touch with his kids before he was six feet under. She thought every cloud had a silver lining. He'd thought her naive. Now damned if she wasn't right.

Here he was dying and yet he couldn't remember a happier time.

He wondered what Caroline would have to say about Cannon and the detective driving up to the Dry Gulch Ranch together. Too late to call her now, but he'd ask her next time she stopped by to check on him. The Bent Pine Ranch wasn't but a few miles away. That was nothing in the country.

R.J. looked up at the sound of rustling grass. A raccoon crawled from beneath the new azalea bushes Hadley had planted to pretty up the front yard. The creature paid no attention to him as it scurried off to hunt for dinner.

R.J. turned and went back into the house. He was tired to the bone, but he doubted sleep would come until Cannon arrived.

Still seemed odd that the detective was taking a vacation while her sister's killer was on the loose. Unless...

Unless she wasn't actually coming for a visit but to pick up Kimmie and take her back to Houston. Cannon might have told a white lie about not having the results to the paternity test. The baby R.J. and the rest of the family were growing so attached to might not be his granddaughter at all.

His heart felt plumb heavy at the thought. Not that he deserved another precious granddaughter after the way he'd neglected his own kids.

He'd been a fool. No one knew that better than him. Too bad it had taken a brain tumor to get his head on straight.

IT WAS A few minutes after ten when Cannon turned onto a narrow back road about five miles from the last sign of civilization.

Brit had spent the past ten minutes finally

trying to explain why they were looking for an isolated farmhouse that might or might not be inhabited by ex-con Melanie Crouch.

"So let me have this straight," Cannon said. "You are out of your jurisdiction, working a case you have been ordered to stay out of, spying on a suspect you have no real evidence to back up your suspicion that she's involved."

"You make that sound like a bad thing."

"Where would I get an idea like that?"

"I can't stay totally out of the case, and not just because I was the one attacked. No homicide detective deserving of the badge would just walk away from an officer's responsibility. And I'm talking about my own sister's murder and an attack on my life.

"Besides, Melanie is a person of interest. She has to be checked out. The department is short staffed due to the money crunch. I'm in the area. It makes sense that I question Melanie, with the local sheriff's knowledge, of course."

"The sheriff you haven't contacted."

"Rick is taking care of that."

"So your partner is in on this?"

"He knows me well enough to know I can't loll around drinking margaritas and watching *Law & Order*."

"No, but if you get fired, you'll have a lot of

time for sipping drinks and watching TV. Can this get you fired?"

"I won't get fired if it goes well."

The chance that it might not go well was what worried Cannon. But he understood her position. He'd do the same in her place. Only, in spite of her claims, she wasn't fully recovered. She needed a few days' rest that he was certain she wasn't going to get.

Still, her business. She was cop. She could take care of herself. She didn't need his protection. That was her job.

So why did he feel so responsible for her now? The woman was seriously getting under his skin, that's why. If he wasn't careful he was going to fall harder for her than he'd ever been thrown in the arena.

"So tell me about Melanie Crouch. What makes her a person of interest?"

"Hers was one of the murder cases I worked after my promotion to Homicide."

"When was that?"

"Three years ago, a few months after my father was murdered. He had been one of the top homicide detectives in the state before becoming the much respected chief of police. There was an outcry from the mayor on down that his killer be caught and prosecuted immediately."

"They must have thought you were the best person to solve the case."

"Either that or it was to honor my father. At any rate, I was the youngest female in Houston to ever make homicide detective."

"And your father's killer?"

"Is yet to be arrested. But I will catch him one day. I will never give up until I do."

The angst-ridden determination in her voice said it all. She couldn't come to grips with having never solved her father's murder. If she didn't bring her sister's murderer to justice, it was going to haunt her forever.

Her heart and soul rested on the outcome of this case.

She was one hell of a woman.

"I'm assuming that Melanie Crouch has reason to have a grudge against you."

"Not a legitimate reason. I was only doing my job. She didn't see it that way."

"So exactly what makes Melanie a person of interest?"

"She was arrested for conspiring to kill her extremely wealthy husband. She hired an assassin to break into their house when she was out of town and kill him in his sleep."

"So she had the perfect alibi."

"In New York with two of her girlfriends."

"And you made the arrest?"

"Yes, but not for several months. I'm sure she thought she was home free by then."

"What led you to her?"

"I can spot fake grief a mile away. It just took time to get enough evidence on her to make the arrest."

"So why is she out of prison so soon after having him killed?"

"She convinced the jury that he'd put her though months of verbal and emotional abuse. She was good at it, too. One day she had half the jury in tears, describing how he told her how stupid she was and blamed her for losing the baby she'd wanted so badly."

"Whatever happened to divorce?"

"Prenups. If she filed for divorce, she got none of his wealth. If he died, she got everything. Unless, of course, she was convicted of killing him. But the jury and the judge sympathized with her and she got a very light sentence which resulted in an early parole."

"When was she paroled?"

"Three weeks ago."

"And she has a history of hiring someone to do her dirty work so you wouldn't have expected her to try to kill you herself."

"Exactly."

"So how does your sister fit into this?"

"That I can't explain, but we have to start somewhere."

"At ten o'clock at night?"

"We're only scouting tonight. We'll save the real action until tomorrow."

Brit directed the beam from a pocket flashlight onto a pencil-drawn map she held in her left hand. "We should pass the shell of a mostly rotted out church in a couple of miles. The spire is still standing. Take the first left turn after that and we should see the old Crouch farmhouse about thirty yards off the road."

"Where did you get this information?"

"From Melanie's parole officer while you were finishing off your steak. Slow down to a crawl when we pass the church. I want to see if the Crouch place looks lived-in. If it's clearly deserted, we might take a look around."

"Why do I feel like we're on a witch hunt?"

"There are no witches in Texas. Maybe a few vampires but definitely no witches."

"Ha-ha."

They reached the standing spire in under five minutes. The moon was bright enough that Cannon had no trouble seeing it or the tombstones stretched out behind it. They hadn't passed a house in several miles. Apparently Melanie's only neighbors were the bodies in the graveyard that stretched behind the church.

"Did you see that?" Brit asked.

"See what?"

"Someone in a long white dress was walking among the graves."

"A vampire?"

"I'm not kidding, Cannon."

"It was probably the moonlight and shadows playing on the old tombstones."

"It was a person. Turn around in Melanie's driveway and go back."

He pulled into the driveway and stopped. "Even if you did see someone—even if it was Melanie—you can't arrest her for being in a graveyard that's right behind her house."

"I'm not going to arrest her. I just want to know what she's doing out there. For all we know, she's burying evidence like the knife that was used on me last night."

"Used on you by a man."

"So? You said yourself he could have had an accomplice. Melanie could have picked him up and driven him out here. He could be inside her house right now."

"Or dead and she's digging his grave," Cannon said, finally getting into the spirit of the hypotheses Brit was coming up with.

A minute later, Cannon had turned around, backtracked and parked his truck in what was once a gravel driveway to the ramshackle old church.

He reached for the pistol he kept beneath his seat. He didn't expect to need it, but he'd take it just in case Brit's illusion turned out to be a flesh-and-blood harbinger of death.

One thing was for certain. If Melanie Crouch was roaming around a graveyard at night burying evidence of bodies, she would not be glad to see them.

Chapter Ten

The truck's headlights cast an eerie glow over the assorted collection of cracked and faded headstones that stretched behind the decrepit church. Brit didn't believe in ghosts, yet the scene made her skin crawl and gooseflesh popped up on her arms.

What she had seen was no illusion though it had looked ethereal. From a distance, the woman had seemed to be floating through the grass, the moonlight painting her wild, flyaway hair in silvery highlights.

At first sight, Brit had feared that her head trauma was dragging her brain back into the murky fog.

But she was thinking clearly now. Logic followed that the woman roaming the ancient cemetery practically in her backyard was Melanie up to no good. Why else would she be out there at this time of night?

The timing for their arrival couldn't have been

better. Brit didn't need a warrant, didn't even need to be on active duty to stop and check out something as suspicious as a woman alone in a deserted cemetery this time of night. If for no other reason, she needed to make sure the stranger wasn't in danger.

Captain Bradford wouldn't buy the story, but she wasn't here.

"Stay in the truck and wait for me," Brit ordered.

"What?" Cannon quipped. "And miss all the fun? Besides, someone has to have your back."

"Then let's go. But I do all the talking if we confront Melanie. And don't pull that gun of yours. That's a direct police order, Cannon Dalton."

"I won't pull it unless the apparition in white pulls a weapon first. That's the best I can promise."

"The woman I saw was no apparition. For the record, I'm as clearheaded as you at the moment."

"That's not saying much. I'm starting to think that driving you away from the hospital this morning is a sign I'm downright crazy."

"Then stay in the truck."

"We've settled that already. Let's go."

She wasn't convinced he believed her, but he didn't hesitate to jump out of his truck and rush around to open her door. Almost as if they were going on a moonlit stroll instead of traipsing through a neglected necropolis looking for a convicted felon who was capable of most anything—like paying someone to kill Brit and Sylvie.

Brit ground her teeth and started walking, more determined than ever to get to the bottom of this. But as the crypts and gravestones grew closer, her nerves grew more ragged, her hands more clammy.

She took out her penlight and shone it on the first tombstone they came to.

James Canton Black, 1894–1935. The only love of Conscience Everett Black. His love was great. His death years too soon. Sin claimed him and took him from me.

"No wonder this place is crumbling and uncared-for," Cannon said. "The bodies planted here have long since returned to dust."

"'Sin claimed him,'" Brit murmured. "I wonder what that means."

"Who knows? There were a lot of superstitions about death in the old days. There still are, I suppose."

Brit kept her eyes peeled for any glimpse of white as they walked among the graves. She didn't see Melanie, but that didn't mean she wasn't nearby, kneeling behind one of the crumbling stone markers, watching and waiting for them to leave so that she could sneak back to her house unnoticed.

They kept walking, listening and searching for any sight or sound that would lead them to Melanie. The wind picked up, blowing wisps of hair into Brit's eyes almost as fast as she could push them away. The temperature seemed to be dropping by the second.

The grass grew higher and thicker as they approached the back of the cemetery, the tombstones almost swallowed up by the overgrowth.

Brit's uneasiness intensified. She felt as if they were treading water, barely staying afloat in the sea of graves. The chill reached deep inside her now.

The scrape of branches at the top of a towering pine raised the hair on the back of her neck. A rustle in the grass stole her breath. A swish of wings above her forced her to swallow an unbidden scream.

She was determined not to let Cannon see how the setting affected her. She could deal with murders and killers on a daily basis without a twinge of dread, but a dark cemetery on the edge of civilization sent icy shivers up her spine.

Brit's foot caught in a vine as she sidestepped a pile of rocks that had probably once marked a grave. Cannon grabbed her arm and pulled her against him to steady her.

An unfamiliar sensation thrummed though her blood. She fought off a crazy desire to cling to him, but instead she pulled away so fast she almost lost her balance again.

"Are you all right?" Cannon asked.

"Just frustrated," she whispered, not willing to admit that his touch had stirred such cravings inside her.

"You don't have to whisper," Cannon said. "You're not going to disturb the inhabitants."

"I might frighten off Melanie."

"If she's nearby, she's hiding, which means she already knows we're here."

"Then let's just keep looking."

His fingers tangled with hers. "Your hand is as cold as ice. You're not letting this place get to you, are you?"

"Of course not," she lied.

"Maybe we should go. My guess is that if it was Melanie you saw, she escaped into the woods that border the cemetery when we drove up. She's likely at home and snuggled into bed by now."

"You're probably right, but I'm not quite ready to give up, not with so many hiding places in every direction. Besides, I keep thinking I'll discover something here to tie her to my attack."

"You mean something like this?"

Brit turned to see what he'd referred to in such an optimistic tone. Even without out her penlight, she could see well enough to realize that they were standing next to a freshly dug grave. Two gold mums rested on top of the mound of earth.

Brit picked up the flowers. "This explains why Melanie was here. She must have left these on the freshly dug grave, a grave she either dug or had dug within the past few hours."

"A very small grave," Cannon noted. "It would be impossible to fit an adult in that hole unless he was butchered into small pieces first."

The blossoms slipped through Brit's fingers and fell to the ground at the sickening image. A wave of vertigo hit again, leaving her dizzy and feeling faint. The last thing she needed now was to pass out.

But she couldn't leave yet. "We have to dig up that grave and see if it holds evidence, like the knife my attacker had planned to kill me with last night."

"Don't you think we should turn that job over to the local sheriff?"

"If we do, chances are that Melanie will move it the second we drive away."

"Then we should call the sheriff now," Cannon said. "Depending on how deep that grave is, it could take hours to unearth whatever's buried there without any proper tools. I think you need to get to bed."

He wrapped an arm around her waist protectively. This time she didn't pull away. For the first time in recent memory she felt as much woman as cop. Hopefully it was just the concussion causing that and not her growing infatuation with Cannon.

She stepped away from the suspicious-looking grave. Something slipped beneath her foot. She stopped to see what she'd stepped on. "It's a shoe," she said, stooping to pull a woman's white leather flip-flop from the grass.

She held it up for scrutiny in the beam of her penlight. "It looks almost new. Melanie must have slipped out of it in her hurry to get away from us."

"That looks like its mate," Cannon said, pointing to a bare, rocky spot a few feet ahead of them. He hurried over to pick it up.

"She's a braver woman I am, if she took off through that wooded area beyond us barefoot and in the dark."

Anxiety hit again as Brit heard a soft footfall behind her followed by the sharp click of a gun being cocked to fire. Before Brit could reach for her weapon, the barrel of what felt like a pistol was pressed into the back of her head.

"Hands in the air, palms open or I shoot. Ladies first."

CANNON DID AS ordered and then spun around. The woman giving the orders and holding the pistol to Brit's head was indeed dressed in a gauzy white nightgown that reached her ankles. Her face was vampire pale. Her hair was long and blond, mussed by the wind.

But it was her eyes that let him know she was capable of pulling the trigger. They had a savage look about them, as if she were ready to punch and devour her prey. This was apparently not the way she had looked at the jury.

"Turn around slowly, Detective," she ordered. "Any quick move by you or your friend will get you killed."

Brit turned around. "You're making a mistake, Melanie. The only thing killing me will do is send you right back to prison."

"Wrong. It would also give me immense satisfaction."

"All I did was my job," Brit said. "You hired a man to kill your husband. If I hadn't arrested you, another police officer would have."

"No other officer was going to arrest me. You were the only one who just wouldn't let it go.

You were never married. You have no idea what it's like to be married to a two-timing, arrogant bastard like Richard Carl Crouch."

"You're right. I've never been married at all. And everyone agrees that he was as arrogant as you claimed. But that's in the past now. You've done your time. You're free to go on with your life now unless you do something as stupid as pulling that trigger."

"What are you doing out here?" Melanie asked, her voice low, her tone spiteful. "You have no right to spy on me."

"We're looking for a friend's ranch," Cannon said, answering for her with the first explanation that came to mind.

"In a cemetery?"

"We saw you roaming the graveyard," Brit said. "We didn't know it was you. We were afraid someone was in trouble."

"You lie. You knew exactly where you were. You came out looking to cause trouble for me. It's not going to work. I've done nothing wrong, but I swear I'll kill you before I let you send me back to that prison."

"Why bother? Just leave it to the man you hired to kill me, or is he dead? Did you pay him all of that money for nothing?"

"I didn't pay anyone a dime to get you. You're not worth it."

"If you don't want to go back to prison, put the gun down, Melanie. It's the only way. Kill me and you'll never see freedom again."

"I won't go back to that prison. I won't." Melanie's voice was rising. She might lose control at any moment and pull that trigger. Cannon lowered his right hand, watching for any chance to catch Melanie off guard long enough for him to go for his own pistol.

"You won't have to go back," Cannon said. "You've paid your time. You have your life back. Don't screw it up. Just hand me the gun and the detective and I will walk away."

"You would, but not the detective. She's already itching to arrest me. Why else would she be out here in the dark of night, roaming around looking for any trace of evidence she can use against me?"

"That's not true," Brit said. "What kind of evidence would I find in a deserted graveyard?"

"I can understand your fears," Cannon said. "I'd probably feel the same in your shoes, but pull that trigger and you lose. This time there will be no early parole. You'll spend the rest of your life in prison. Revenge can't be worth that to you."

"I may go to prison but Detective Garner will go straight to hell."

A pinecone dropped from the branches of the

towering pine just behind Melanie, startling her. She spun around. In that split second, Cannon pulled his gun and stepped in front of Brit.

"Drop your gun, Melanie."

She stared at him, her eyes leveled at him like a laser.

Brit stepped from behind him, weapon in hand now and pointed at Melanie. "No way can you kill us both before we kill you. Is a split second of revenge worth your life?"

A motor sounded in the background and suddenly the area was bathed in flashing blue lights. From the periphery of his vision Cannon saw that a police car had pulled onto the property and was bouncing across the rocky ground toward them.

Melanie hurled the gun into the maze of tombstones and took off like a bolt of lightning, her bare feet flying across the rocks and grass and heading for the wooded area between her house and the graveyard.

The gun hit a stone marker and ricocheted back toward them, fortunately not going off.

Instinctively, Cannon raced after Melanie. He caught up with her just as she reached the edge of the clearing. He grabbed her arm and pulled her to a halt. Seconds later, Brit and two armed officers of the law were at his side.

"Get your hands off me," Melanie said,

throwing in a few four-letter expletives to make her point.

"Watch your mouth," the older lawman ordered. "One more tirade out of you and I'll throw you into jail for disturbing the peace if nothing else. And you can unhand her," he said to Cannon. "If she tries to run again, I'll handle the situation."

Cannon let go of her arm. She backed away from him but didn't run.

"Now would someone tell me what the devil is going on here?"

Brit flashed her ID. "I'm Detective Brittany Garner with the Houston Police Department."

"Who are you?" he asked, pointing a finger a Cannon.

"Cannon Dalton."

"Cannon Dalton." He scratched his whiskered chin. "Name sounds right familiar. You look a little familiar, too. I'm guessing you're the bull-riding son of R.J. Dalton."

"I am." There was obviously no way of keeping that a secret in this part of Texas.

"The woman he was chasing is Melanie Crouch, recently released from prison."

"I know Melanie," he assured Brit. "I'm Walter Garcia, sheriff of this county. My deputy here is Bobby Blaxton."

"I don't know what brought you out here

tonight, but your timing couldn't have been better," Brit said.

"I had business in the area, and you're a long way from home, Detective. Mind telling me why you're chasing one of my citizens through a graveyard this time of night?"

Brit explained the situation as succinctly as possible, stressing that they had no intention of doing anything other than to check out the Crouch place before talking to the sheriff the following morning.

"Detective Garner pinned one crime on me. Now she's looking to do the same thing again," Melanie argued, her voice calm and measured.

"If all you were doing was checking out the house, exactly why were you here in the cemetery?" the sheriff asked Brit.

"We glimpsed a woman running through the deserted cemetery," Brit said. "I had no way of knowing if it was Melanie, but I felt it important to ascertain that no one was in danger."

"Is that a fact? Looked like you were chasing her when I showed up."

"Only after she sneaked out from behind one of the tombstones and pulled a gun on us," Cannon explained. He reached down and picked up the gun with two fingers, careful not to smudge the fingerprints.

"I'll take that," the sheriff said.

Cannon handed it off gingerly.

"A gun, huh?" the sheriff said. "Sounds like you got some explaining to do, too, Miss Melanie. How come you have a weapon on you when the specifications of your parole specifically prohibit it?"

"It's for my own protection. A single woman living alone this far out in the country has to have protection."

The sheriff hiked up his trousers and then nudged his Stetson a little lower on his forehead. "If you're so worried about your safety, what are you doing out in this abandoned cemetery this time of night?"

"I buried a kitten out here earlier today. I was visiting the grave. Brought her some flowers I picked up in Oak Grove today."

"You haven't been out of prison but a few weeks. You telling me you got yourself a cat that already up and died on you?"

"I didn't get a cat. Some jerk threw a sack full of kittens out of a truck and left them in the woods to die. I took them in. One didn't make it."

"Can't see any way we're going to get to the bottom of this tonight," the sheriff drawled. "Besides, it'll be pushing midnight by the time I get home and to bed as it is. Cannon, are you and the detective here staying at the Dry Gulch?"

"For now," he admitted.

"Then I'll be out to the ranch in the morning to have a chat with you both. I been wanting to get there to check on R.J., anyway. Might as well kill two birds with one stone."

"In the meantime, what's to keep Melanie from going on the run as soon as we leave?" Brit asked.

"A jail cell. I'm hauling her in for breaking parole by having possession of a firearm."

Melanie uttered a few more curses. "You don't have any proof that's my gun."

"My suspicions and the detective's word is all I need for you to enjoy a stay in the clinker for the next twenty-four hours."

"I can live with that," Brit said.

Garcia fitted the handcuffs around Melanie's wrists.

"You and Dalton go home and get some sleep. I'll be there before noon tomorrow."

Cannon was pleased to take the sheriff's advice. Rest was exactly what Brit needed. He was beginning to fade, himself, now that Melanie was in cuffs.

Within minutes they were on their way to the Dry Gulch Ranch and R.J. The dread swelled again. He was certain the reunion was a mistake. By the time he drove up to the rambling old house, he was sure of it.

Chapter Eleven

Brit rolled down her window as they approached the house. The temperature had dropped a few degrees and a chill crept deep inside her as she studied her new surroundings.

Clouds had rolled in over the past half hour, obscuring the stars and the moon, outlining the house in shades of grisly gray. Intimidating shadows from towering trees stalked the gables and chimneys. The porch swing swayed and creaked in the wind as if occupied by a hostile aberration that resented their intrusion.

Perhaps arriving at this time of night had not been the best of ideas, especially with Cannon already dreading spending the night under his father's roof.

She rolled up her window and opened her door as Cannon shifted into Park and killed the engine. Fatigue washed over her again as her feet hit the driveway. A good night's sleep without incident and they might both feel differently.

Her sizzling attraction to Cannon might cool. He might decide he'd had enough of playing nurse and driver to her.

With their two duffel bags swinging from his shoulder, Cannon extended a supportive hand to the curve of her back as she climbed the steps to the wide front porch. He was clearly good at playing the protective role. He might find a way to get away from her quickly when she returned to the tough, in-your-face, risk-taking cop she was normally.

But for now his effect on her was showing no signs of weakening. Spending the night under the same roof might make the unwelcome desires more potent.

Cannon turned the doorknob. The door squeaked open. The dim light of a lamp welcomed them inside. One look around and Brit's foreboding concerning the house vanished.

Hot coals glistened in the giant stone fireplace. Crocheted throws rested on the leather couch and comfortable chairs. A bouquet of fall flowers in a white pottery vase adorned a pine side table, its fragrance blending with the smell of spices.

A pair of wire reading glasses rested on the pages of an opened magazine. A nearby shelf was filled with books of all sizes, except for the top shelf which held framed snapshots. Many were in black and white, the subjects dressed in attire from throughout the former century.

A stunning watercolor of a majestic cinnamon-colored steed ridden by a man in a black cowboy hat, a Western shirt and a pair of shiny black cowboy boots hung above the fireplace.

"It's exactly as I've always imagined these old ranch houses to look," she whispered.

"Old and outdated?" Cannon questioned, not bothering to hide the fact that he didn't like being here.

That was especially strange since she felt as if she were coming home even though she'd never lived outside the city of Houston. "The house has a strong sense of continuity between the past and the present," she said.

Cannon shrugged his shoulders. "Not my past."

"I wouldn't bet on that." She walked over and picked up one of the framed black-and-white photos of an older man. "You have a definite resemblance to this man. He could be your grandfather or at least an ancestor."

"Still would be a stranger to me. Let's check out the guest room—unless you're hungry. R.J. said to help ourselves to leftovers, including pecan pie made with Dry Gulch pecans."

"Hard to turn down temptation like that."

"I would have thought you capable of resisting any kind of temptation, Detective."

A blush burned her cheeks. His teasing too closely edged the truth. But she wouldn't be intimidated by his flirtatious comment. "I can," she agreed, "but I don't always want to."

"Nice to know."

She returned the picture to the shelf and started down the hallway, stopping at the first open door. Again, she was enchanted by the inviting aura of the room. The furnishings were softened by the glow of lamplight. A colorful quilt was pulled down on the king-size bed, revealing a nest of tempting white sheets just waiting to be crawled between.

"It has an adjoining bath," Cannon said, pointing to a door that had been left ajar. "R.J. assured me he'd leave fresh towels out for you."

"I hate that I've put him out."

"If you did, you'd have never guessed by his reaction. He sounded like he was excited to have company."

"I'm sure that you're the one he's excited to see."

"No doubt. One more offspring on which to assuage his guilt."

They left the bedroom and followed the dimly lit hallway to the back of the house. The kitchen was on the left. Cannon reached inside the door, flipped the switch and flooded the space with light.

The focal point was a large marred and well-worn oak table. Brit could easily imagine the large Dalton family gathered around the table, eating, laughing and talking.

Exactly the kind of place she'd imagined her friends had experienced when they'd gone to their grandparents for Thanksgiving and Christmas. Her family had been only her mother and father up until her mother had died when Brit was twelve.

After that it had been just her and her dad. He'd always made a special attempt to spend holidays with her, but that didn't always work out. When it didn't, she'd be invited to the McIntosh's. Aidan McIntosh had been her dad's partner and best friend. Louise McIntosh had been like a second mother to her until the terrible night of Aidan's arrest.

This was not the time to revisit that night in her mind.

Cannon opened the refrigerator and started lifting plastic tops to peek inside the containers. "Looks like some kind of potato casserole, cold fried chicken, field peas and a few slices of hothouse tomatoes. If that doesn't do it for you, there're eggs and I'd wager I can find some bacon or sausage to go with them."

She reached past him and retrieved the pie. "I have mine," she teased. "It's every man for himself."

"And after I've faced the fierce arm of the law for you."

"I suppose I could share a bite or two."

"How about a glass of milk to wash it down?"

"Now you're talking, cowboy."

In minutes, they were at the table, relishing the best pecan pie she'd ever tasted. Even Cannon seemed to be relaxing in the cozy warmth of the kitchen.

"How did you ever get into something as suicidal as bull riding?" she asked.

"Nothing suicidal about it. I work damn hard to stay alive."

"Exactly. So why not become a doctor or attorney or even a regular rancher like R.J.?"

"The thought never entered my mind. I moved to my uncle's ranch out in West Texas when I was thirteen. Rodeo was the most exciting thing going around there, and we had no shortage of bulls."

"Wasn't your mother terrified you'd get hurt?"

"She was killed in a boating accident. That's why I ended up on my uncle's ranch."

So they had both lost their mother at an early age. That might be the only thing they had in common.

Brit let the subject drop and turned the talk to the totally impersonal subject of the latest political scandal. The minutes flew by as they talked, joked and enjoyed the pie.

"You'd best get some sleep," Cannon said once they'd finished their midnight snack and rinsed their dishes. "Tomorrow promises to be another action-packed day, starting with your meeting with Sheriff Garcia."

"I am beat," she said truthfully. "But still feeling one hundred percent better than I did this morning."

"Not because you followed the doctor's orders."

"How can you say that? I slept all afternoon and during the drive here from Houston. Except for my brief foray into the land of the dead and deranged I was a perfect patient."

"I wouldn't say perfect. And you definitely ignored your boss's demands."

"You would have to bring that up. I'll deal with her when the time comes—if it comes. She won't argue with success." And after experiencing Melanie's emotional state firsthand, Brit was convinced she was their most credible suspect to date, though she still couldn't figure out how Melanie would have known that Sylvie was Brit's sister.

They left the kitchen and went back down

the hallway, stopping at the open door that led to the guest room.

Brit looked up at Cannon. "Where will you sleep?"

He met her gaze. His eyes were questioning, as if he were pondering whether that might be an invitation to share her bed. The tension sparked to the point of explosion.

Brit trembled as the possibility of falling asleep in his strong arms filled her senses. She took a deep breath and tamped down the unbidden desire.

"I'm told there are several guest rooms upstairs to choose from," Cannon said. "But I'll be close by. If you need anything, anything at all, just call and I can be here in seconds."

"I'll be fine," she said. "The room is so cozy and I'm so tired, I may fall asleep with my clothes on."

He lingered, then took a step closer, leaning in so that his lips were mere inches from hers. Her heart skipped crazily. Her head felt light. Her stomach fluttered.

She knew she should back away, but her body ignored her brain. She lifted her mouth to his and then dissolved into a deliciously sweet eruption of passion as his lips found hers.

His lips were soft at first, then more demanding. The thrill of their mingling breaths rocked though her like fire. The inhibitions that had become part of her being melted away and she kissed him back, letting the thrill of him wash though her.

The unexpected hunger for him was primal, untamed. Her arms slid around his neck, pulling him closer as her body arched toward his.

When he had the good sense to pull away, her body went weak.

"Don't think the doctor would approve of this." His voice was a husky whisper.

"Probably not," she agreed, though it wasn't her physical health she was worried about but her inability to control her emotions where Cannon was concerned. It wasn't the time or the place. Likely not even the right man, no matter how right it felt right now.

"Good night, Detective."

"Good night, cowboy."

She stood in the door for what seemed an eternity, drowning in the ecstasy.

One thing about Cannon Dalton. When he kissed, a woman knew she'd been kissed.

CANNON SLEPT RESTLESSLY, waking when the thunderstorm went through and several times since, agonizing over the situation he'd fallen into.

Kimmie.

The murder of Kimmie's mother.

The attempt on Brit's life.

The kiss that never should have happened. The kiss that had sent him on a fast track to heaven. The kiss he ached to repeat.

He finally gave up on sleep when the first light of dawn crept through his open second-floor window. He slipped from beneath the covers, surprised to find an icy chill to the air.

He padded to the window in his bare feet, naked, the way he always woke. He hadn't owned a pair of pajamas since he'd left his uncle's ranch at eighteen. He'd always showered before hitting the sack and liked letting everything hang free while he slept.

He stared into the purplish haze of dawn and spotted the first frost of the season, a thin layer of ice that clung to the blades of grass like sugar frosting.

The house was quiet, but the odor of fresh-brewing coffee tantalized his senses. Might as well go down and get his encounter with R.J. over with. Hopefully, he could avoid a barrage of questions about how he planned to take care of Kimmie if the test turned out positive.

And he definitely didn't want to discuss his reasons for not buying into the controlling stipulations of R.J.'s will and becoming one of the Dry Gulch Ranch entourage of followers. But he wouldn't lie to R.J. or pretend to have any interest in moving out here to watch him die.

Cannon slipped into his jeans, shirt, socks and boots and made his way to the kitchen. The light on the automatic coffeepot was green, but there was no sign of life.

Cannon checked the pot. It was programmed to start perking at six o'clock. It was six-ten now, so R.J. would probably come to the kitchen for his morning jolt of caffeine soon.

Cannon took a mug from the cabinet and filled it with the pungent brew. Still restless, he took his coffee outside. The household might be sleeping but the rest of creation was waking up.

Horses neighed. Birds sang and darted among the branches of oaks, sycamores and pines. A bullfrog croaked. A wasp buzzed by his head. Wide-open spaces stretched out over the pasture and to the wooded area beyond.

A man could get used to this life right quick, he thought as he started down a well-worn trail that led away from the back of the house. Waking up at the Dry Gulch intensified his anticipation for the day he had enough money to buy his own ranch and start raising rodeo stock.

And not just any rodeo stock. He aimed to provide the best animals in the business. His bulls and broncs would be the ones the cowboys prayed they'd get to ride, the ones who could guarantee a rider top points if he could stay on his full eight seconds.

Cannon had his future planned to the nth degree.

At least he had until this week. So much for a man's plans when life decided to kick him around. First Kimmie. Now this crazy reaction to Brit. The detective was doing a hell of a job on him. If he wasn't careful, he'd start believing the two of them could make a go of it even though they weren't even heading in the same direction.

He shouldn't have kissed her. She shouldn't have let him. But she hadn't just let him, she'd kissed him back. Now she was taking over his mind. If this was love, fate was playing a rotten trick on him.

Brit was so dedicated to her job that, according to Captain Bradford, she never even took a vacation. That meant living in Houston. He was a bull rider who was always on the road. And when he did settle down, he planned to do it on a ranch.

Their lifestyle differences weren't the worst of it. He might be the father of her twin sister's baby. A baby conceived during a one-night stand with a woman he barely remembered and had never had any real feelings for.

Brit's bitterness over that had been obvious in their first meeting. So had her contempt for his career choice. That bitterness might be shoved to the back burner now but it would resurface when the urgency of the moment faded.

It was preposterous to even dream they could make it as a couple.

But damn, that kiss had carried a wallop. He could still feel it right down to his toes. How in the hell could he ever trust himself around her now?

He turned and walked back toward the old ranch house and the mouthwatering odor of frying bacon. When he reached the back porch, he heard a babble of voices he didn't recognize. Talking. Laughing.

All suddenly interrupted by the wail of a baby. A baby who might be his own flesh and blood. If she was, life was about to come falling down on top of him like trees in a West Texas tornado. If the lab didn't call with results soon, he was going to pop like a cheap balloon.

He said a few curses under his breath, opened the door and stepped inside to face the posse of Daltons who'd obviously arrived while he was taking his walk.

BRIT WOKE TO the clattering vibration of her phone on the bedside table. She reached for it, then hesitated, her mind so lost in the dregs of a deep sleep she didn't know where she was.

Rectangles of sunlight sneaked around and through the slits of opaque blinds. A strange bed. A strange room. Frosty air flowing through an open window.

The Dry Gulch Ranch.

With Cannon Dalton.

How could that have slipped her mind even for a second? Her lips tingled at the memory of his kiss. The momentary confusion lifted as the thrill of it rushed through her veins.

She slid her finger across the phone to take the call. "Hello."

"Did I wake you?"

"Yeah, but that's okay. What time is it?"

"Almost eight. Are you okay?"

"Of course. I'm fine."

"You don't sound too great and you're usually in the office and on your second espresso by now."

"I was kept up half the night by a thunderstorm that has apparently moved on. And I was ordered to stay out of the office, remember?"

"You were also ordered off the case, but you're not complying with that."

"Not until the lunatic who killed Sylvie and tried to kill me is behind bars. Did you locate Hagan?"

"No. Best source of information indicates he's in Mexico."

"What about Palmer?"

"He's agreed to come in and answer a few questions this morning at nine—with his new sleazy lawyer, of course. After that, I've decided I should head north to a chat with Melanie Crouch."

"That would be a waste of time since I'm already here."

"Don't tell me you drove up there last night in the condition you were in?"

"No. Cannon drove me."

"Cannon Dalton?"

"He's the only Cannon I know."

"Correction, partner. You don't actually know him. You just met him. All you know about him is that he knocked up your sister who was later murdered."

"He had nothing to do with her murder."

"You can't be sure of that."

"Of course I can. I have a sixth sense about guilt. You know that. Anyway, Bradford said I should get out of town and take a few days off. I decided to spend that time with Kimmie."

"So you and Cannon are at his father's ranch. Easy to see how he moved in on your sister so fast. The guy doesn't waste any time."

"He is just being helpful." Easier for Brit to see how her sister fell for him so fast. A good reminder for her to slow down in the romance department. Now to convince her libido of that.

"It's fine by me if you talk to Melanie," Rick said. "But there will be hell to pay if you blatantly ignore Bradford's order. It could even cost you your job."

"I'll talk to her. When she realizes I'm fine, she'll come around. Is she in the office now?"

"Yep."

"What kind of mood is she in?"

"The chief of police was in her office a few minutes ago and they both were frowning."

"Then I'll call and preface my offer to question Melanie Crouch with a reminder of how short staffed and overworked Homicide is."

"What about the headaches from the concussion?"

"Totally gone."

"And the disorientation?"

"Also gone." Thankfully, that was true, at least for now.

"Good. What I called to tell you should make you feel even better."

"Hit me."

"We have an ID on your attacker."

She sat up in bed, her interest intensifying. "Who?"

"A guy named Clive Austin."

"Doesn't sound familiar."

"He goes by Stats. Have no idea why."

"Still doesn't mean anything. Did I arrest him?"

"No, nor did your father. But Stats does have a rap sheet that would stretch around Reliant Center. Mostly in Austin and Dallas."

"What kind of crimes?"

"Started off with shoplifting when he was a preteen. Graduated early to hot checks, burglary and then moved on to armed robbery."

"But he isn't in jail?"

"Not at the present time. His last arrest was in Tyler, Texas, for some elaborate scam to bilk money out of aging widows. He got out of prison on a technicality nine months ago. Word has it he moved back to Dallas and has the mob on his tail for a huge unpaid tab with his bookie."

"No record of murder for hire?"

"No, but there's always a first time for career criminals like him, especially if he needed money."

"Which he obviously does."

"You got it. Now we just need to find out who hired him."

"All the more reason I should be the one to talk to Melanie while you check out other suspects. I can be in her face before you get out of Dallas morning traffic."

"Bradford will insist you keep this by the book and go through the local sheriff."

"I already have. More reason for me to handle this."

She explained the graveyard encounter and how it had ended with the sheriff's snapping a bracelet on Melanie and carting her off to jail.

"So now Cannon's not only your chauffeur and nurse, but also he's involved in the investigation?"

Rick's tone left no question as to how he felt about that development.

"It wasn't planned, Rick. We were only going to drive by Melanie's house when we spotted her in the cemetery."

"Bradford will be royally pissed if she hears about this."

"There's no reason for her to hear it, at least not yet. With luck, not ever. Now if we've covered everything, I need to get some coffee and call Bradford."

"Call me back as soon as you talk to her so I can plan my day."

"Right."

Once the connection was broken, Brit threw her legs over the side of the bed. The quick movement delivered a sharp pain through her right shoulder and down her arm.

The soreness from the attack seemed more

painful today than yesterday or else she was just paying more attention to it now that the headache was gone.

The only consolation was that if she felt this sore, Clive Austin must be in worse shape. He'd lost a lot of blood and apparently hadn't shown up at a hospital. If he had, Rick would have mentioned it.

Paid to kill her. But by whom? Melanie? More important, how did either of them know she and Sylvie were sisters? Would the killing stop now that she'd wounded her attacker or would that only further enrage the person who'd hired Clive?

Brit heard footsteps and voices coming from down the hall. Probably R.J. and Cannon getting reacquainted but possibly the sheriff who might have decided to pop in earlier than he'd indicated.

Luckily she'd showered last night, so all she had to do was slip into some clothes, brush her hair and join them.

If it wasn't the sheriff, she'd say good morning, get her coffee and then come back to her room and give the captain a call. Better to deal with her after caffeine.

After that, she'd seek out Kimmie. She must be somewhere on the ranch and Brit couldn't wait to see her adorable niece.

But it was Cannon and last night's burning kiss that haunted her mind as she dressed in a pair of black pants and a pale blue sweater.

Boundaries, she reminded herself as she brushed a stain of blush to her cheeks and smoothed her lips with pink gloss. Not only to preserve her professionalism but also to protect her heart.

Determined to keep that in mind, she followed the voices to the kitchen. Her breath caught in her throat when her gaze rested on Cannon.

He was dressed in jeans, a Western shirt and his boots. A heart-stopping hunk of masculinity holding a smiling, gurgling Kimmie in his arms.

Brit's willpower to keep her infatuation in check melted faster than a chip of ice in a sauna.

Shaken by the intensity of her reaction to seeing him with Kimmie, she stepped away from the door before anyone noticed her. Perhaps it was best to call Bradford first. That should cool off the heat Cannon had generated.

She tiptoed back to her room and made the call. Unfortunately, Sheriff Garcia had called Bradford first. The captain was ready to have her head, and Cannon was the source of her rage.

Chapter Twelve

"Don't be nervous," Faith encouraged. "You'll get the hang of this in no time."

The assurance did nothing to ease Cannon's fears. He was afraid he was holding Kimmie too tight. Or not tight enough. Or not supporting her head in just the right way. Or that she was going to start wailing.

As if on cue, Kimmie started to fret.

"Either I'm doing something wrong or she doesn't like me."

"Try holding her on your shoulder and patting her gently on the back. She may need to burp."

"Burping. Now that's an art I can probably teach her. How do I get her to my shoulder?"

Faith smiled as she helped him readjust his positioning of the wiggly infant.

To Cannon's amazement, Kimmie burped, a good loud one. "Now we're getting somewhere. But you know, we're jumping the gun here with all this parenting practice. I still don't have the lab results."

"I don't need DNA to know this is your daughter, Cannon. She has your eyes and coloring. And she has the Dalton mouth—a crooked twist to her lips when she smiles."

"C'mon. All babies look like this."

"Absolutely not. Look at any of your pictures when you and your half brothers were babies. Hard to tell one of you from the other."

Cannon wasn't interested in Dalton family photos and he didn't see the likeness to him. But he had to admit, Kimmie was growing on him. She'd obviously already captured Faith's heart.

Faith was Travis's wife, one of the many members of the Dalton clan who'd stopped by for a cup of coffee and to say hello this morning after Leif and Joni had arrived with Kimmie and before rushing off to their own lives.

Apparently news had spread quickly that Cannon and Brit were spending the night at the ranch, though he'd gotten the feeling that stopping by the big house for coffee and/or breakfast was routine for most of them.

Faith was the only visitor still here, apparently Kimmie's caretaker for the morning. Perhaps R.J.'s, too. They all seemed to keep close tabs on the father who had never been around for any of them.

At least that was the distinct impression Cannon had gotten at the reading of the will where R.J. had surprised them with the manipulative stipulations and the fact that he wasn't dead. Not a one of his half siblings had been singing the old man's praises that day.

Adam hadn't even stayed around for beer, barbecue and a tour of the ranch. Yet he was the first one to move onto the ranch with his wife and two twin daughters. He was managing all of the daily operations of the ranch now.

Kimmie's good mood was short-lived. She puckered her lips and started to whimper. "I think she knows she's in shaky hands," Cannon said.

"She'll get used to you," R.J. said. "You might as well get used to her, too. If that test comes back positive, as Faith and Kimmie's detective aunt Brit seem convinced that it will, you'll be her only parent."

As if Cannon needed that reminder, especially by R.J., a man who hadn't cared about fatherly responsibilities until he found out he was dying.

Cannon picked up one of Kimmie's toys and rattled it for her. She quit fussing and her eyes opened wide. Finally, something she liked. She waved her tiny fists, cooing as if she were trying to tell him something.

He wasn't ready to try his hand at baby talk,

certainly not in front of Faith and R.J., but he couldn't deny a tug at his heart. Kind of like when he'd first moved to his uncle's ranch and watched a new spindly-legged colt come into the world. Only this time the pleasure was mixed with anxiety.

Kimmie was going to need a real father, one who could change her diapers and bathe and dress her. One who knew what to do when she cried. One who knew about formula and baby food and immunizations.

Cannon wasn't that man.

He shifted and spied Brit standing in the doorway. It hit him again how stunning she was without even trying. No heavy makeup. No fancy clothes. Just a natural beauty.

The thrill of last night's kiss shot through his senses. He did his best to tamp down his arousal before it became embarrassing.

Their gazes met. It wasn't desire he saw there, but the cop toughness she'd greeted him with two nights ago when he'd shown up at her precinct. He wondered if there had been some new development in the case overnight, but he couldn't broach the subject in front of Faith and Dalton.

"Good morning," Brit said as she joined them in the kitchen and walked over to plant a kiss among the wispy curls on the top of Kimmie's head. "And good morning to you, little angel."

Cannon handed the baby to her without hesitation. To his surprise, Brit was almost as awkward with Kimmie as he was. Nonetheless, she cuddled the infant in the curve of her arm and Kimmie seemed content—at least for the time being.

"I didn't mean to sleep so late," Brit apologized.

"Don't you worry about that," R.J. said. "The storm probably kept you up half the night. It did me, not that I don't always wake up a half-dozen times every night."

"I usually have that same problem, but I slept soundly once the storm passed." She walked over and offered her free hand to R.J. "I'm Detective Brit Garner. We met briefly when I dropped Kimmie off the other day."

"Yep. Glad you're sticking around a little longer this time."

"I apologize for my abruptness, but at the time I was afraid you'd refuse to accept responsibility for Kimmie, and I was neck-deep in a very important murder case."

"Kimmie's mother?"

"Yes, I suppose Cannon explained that situation to you."

"Not in any detail. He mentioned it last night when you were driving up. That's all."

"There's not much more to tell just yet," Brit said. "The investigation is ongoing."

The woman who'd been giving Cannon tips on handling Kimmie stepped closer to Brit. "I'm Faith, Travis Dalton's wife."

"Nice to meet you," Brit said. "Thanks so much for helping care for Kimmie."

"I should be thanking you. It's so much fun to have a baby in the house. But Hadley has done more caretaking than I have. The rest of us have to threaten rebellion to get Kimmie away from her."

"I'm sure Kimmie is thriving on all the attention."

"I'm sorry about your sister," Faith said. "So sad for Kimmie to lose her mother before she ever got to know her. I'm sure it must be difficult for you to deal with the grief and the investigation at the same time."

"I think it would be more difficult if I didn't have the investigation to focus on."

"You did the right thing bringing Kimmie here," R.J. said. "Having my youngest granddaughter around is better than any medicine my doctor prescribes."

"I'm glad to hear that, and I really appreciate you letting me visit her."

"Stay as long as you like. Always room for one or a dozen more at the Dry Gulch. Long as I got a biscuit, you got half."

"Now that's hospitality."

Faith walked over and set a mug of hot coffee on the table near Brit.

"Thanks. You must have been reading my mind."

"No, but I know how worthless I am until I have that first cup of coffee in the morning. How about some breakfast? We had blueberry pancakes and sausage if you'd like that."

"Please don't go to that much trouble."

"It's no trouble at all. I can warm the leftover sausage patties and the pancake batter is already mixed. All I have to do is spoon some on the griddle."

"If you turn down the blueberry pancakes, you'll be missing a real treat," Cannon warned. "In fact, I'll do the cooking while you reconnect with Kimmie."

"Now that's an offer I can't refuse."

Watching her with Kimmie, Cannon wondered why Brit hadn't married and had children of her own. It definitely couldn't be that she hadn't had plenty of men to choose from.

Might just be that she'd chosen a career over family. From the little he'd seen her job didn't seem to leave a lot of time for marriage or babies. Or even for recuperating from an attack.

Or had she simply not met Mr. Right yet?

Scared of where his own thoughts were heading, Cannon forced himself to concentrate on cooking pancakes. He stirred the batter while the griddle was heating. At least Brit had agreed to eat. That must mean the nausea hadn't come back.

Just thinking about the attack sent the anxiety bucking around inside him again. Her life was still in danger.

She was the cop. She had her own gun. She was the protector and would balk at any suggestion she needed protecting. The only reason she was hanging out with him was that she'd needed a driver until she was back to one hundred percent fighting form.

From the looks of things, that was probably now.

He wasn't sure when he'd started thinking otherwise, but he was sure what he was feeling right now. No matter when the lab work came back or what the result, he wasn't going anywhere until he was sure Brit was safe.

R.J. SETTLED IN a kitchen chair. He hadn't done much talking this morning, but he'd done a whole lot of watching and listening. He hadn't quite figured out what Brit and Cannon were doing here together, but he knew there was something cooking between them.

Anyone with half a brain could see that in the way they looked at each other. R.J. was mighty curious how that came about considering Cannon was the father of her dead sister's baby. Had sure sounded as though he wasn't in her good graces when she'd dropped Kimmie off at the ranch.

Couldn't predict love. It had a way of sneaking up on you without your seeing it coming. Had happened to Leif and Travis and it was working great for them. If Cannon and Brit pulled it off, it would sure be a blessing for little Kimmie.

God's plan, his neighbor Caroline would say.

But R.J. was betting they hadn't driven out here pushing midnight last night just to spend some time with Kimmie this morning, not with the detective still trying to find her sister's killer. R.J. had better sense than to go meddling into that, too. Besides, life had a way of sifting out the weevils if you gave it time.

He leaned back in the kitchen chair. "Never met a female homicide detective before. What made you decide to take on a grisly job like that?"

"My father was a homicide detective before

he became the chief of police. He was my idol. I always wanted to grow up and be just like him."

"Must be a good man?"

"He *was*. He was murdered three years ago. I made detective a few months later. I think the promotion was as much out of respect for him as for me, but I love the job. Not the murders, but bringing the guilty to justice."

"Did you find your dad's killer?"

"Not yet, but I will."

"My money's on you," R.J. said. "You ever do any horseback riding?"

"Not lately."

"Might want to try it sometime. I always think clearest on the back of a horse, especially since that tumor started playing havoc with my thinking skills. Life just looks more manageable from the saddle."

"That's an interesting theory. I'd love to test it when I have more time."

"You're always welcome to ride one of my animals. I got some real beauties in the horse barn. You should at least take a walk out to see them while you're here."

"I'd love to do that."

"Catch me at a good time and I'll go with you."

Cannon brought over a plate of pancakes and sausages and set them in front of Brit.

Faith put the syrup and silverware on the table and refilled Brit's coffee mug. "Let me take Kimmie for you while you eat."

"I think you'd better. Wouldn't want to drip syrup on her."

Before she had the first bite down, the doorbell rang.

"I'll get that," R.J. said. "Probably just a neighbor stopping by to say howdy. You keep right on eating."

R.J. took his time shuffling down the hallway. Whoever it was he planned to get rid of them fast. He was hoping for some one-on-one time with Cannon this morning.

He opened the door, surprised to see Sheriff Garcia standing there.

"What brings you out this time of the morning? Got trouble out this way?"

"I just left Ben Campbell's spread. Connie Barrick's son got drunk again last night, ran off the road and rammed through Ben's fence. Car's still sitting there. Back wheels are buried in the muddy ditch. Found Jack Barrick sleeping it off under a tree."

"Ben have any livestock wander off?"

"Nope. Fortunately, all his cattle were grazing in other pastures."

"Well, you're here, might as well come in and have a cup of coffee," R.J. offered reluctantly.

"Coffee will have to wait. I'm here to see Detective Garner."

"What about?"

"Police business. Didn't she tell you I was coming?"

"No, but then we hadn't a chance to do much talking yet. She's just now having breakfast."

"Well, go get her. We got business to discuss—in private."

"Why don't you come on back to the kitchen with me and have a cup of coffee while she finishes her pancakes?"

"I'll have coffee after we talk."

"I'm sure whatever you have to say can wait five more minutes."

"I say we let her decide that. Just tell her that another body connected to her investigation just hit the morgue."

Chapter Thirteen

"What does he mean another body in the morgue?"

"I have no idea, Cannon. I'm just telling you what Sheriff Garcia said. He talked like it would mean something to Brit."

Cannon picked up his pace to keep up with Brit, then grabbed her arm and tugged her to a stop. He looked around quickly, making sure that neither Faith nor R.J. had followed them down the narrow hallway.

"I think you should reconsider talking to Melanie. Let someone else handle this case. Take the day off and spend it with Kimmie."

"I'm fine, Cannon. I'm a cop. I don't run from murders. I find the killers and lock them up."

"When you're healthy. You're not yet."

"I'll handle this, Cannon. I don't tell you how to ride a bull. You can't tell me how to do my job. I'll listen to what the sheriff has to say and then I'll call Rick back and see why he didn't tell me this."

"Call Rick *back?*"

"He called this morning. They have an ID on my attacker. If there had been another murder attributed to him, I'm sure he would have told me."

"Who's the assailant?"

"A man named Clive Austen."

"How is he connected to you?"

"He's not, or at least not that I know of. I've never even heard of him, but apparently he has an impressive rap sheet in the Dallas area. Anything for money except work for it."

"So if Melanie is behind this, she might have just followed her usual modus operandi even though it didn't work for her before."

"That's a definite possibility."

"Do they have an address on this Austin guy?"

"I don't know. Look, Cannon, Rick's not the only one I talked to this morning. I also called Captain Bradford."

"And she didn't mention another victim, either?"

"No, but she had plenty to say about you. I've been ordered not to discuss this case with you and definitely not to get you involved the way I did last night at the graveyard."

"How did she find out about that?"

"Sheriff Garcia called her this morning. Apparently they've worked together before and he wanted to clear up a few questions about my wanting to interrogate Melanie. Bradford was furious—even more about your being with me than the fact that I'd ignored her orders not to get involved."

Cannon shrugged. "I walked with you through a graveyard."

"And encountered a suspect in an active investigation. End result, I am not to interrogate Melanie Crouch today or any other day."

Cannon mumbled a curse under his breath, but he let go of Brit's arm. He hadn't seen that coming but probably should have. Now he'd screwed things up for her. Of course, if he'd let her go into the graveyard without backup, she might be dead. Someone should point that out to Captain Bradford.

"I'd like to be with you when you talk to the sheriff."

"Not going to happen, Cannon. Bradford will yank my rank if I go against her orders on this. Just back off."

Instead, he followed her onto the porch. The

sheriff was leaning against a support post. Travis Dalton was climbing the steps. Cannon recognized him from the reading of the will.

"Good morning, Sheriff," Travis said. "What's up?"

Garcia nodded toward Brit and Cannon. "I've got business with Detective Garner. I guess you two have met."

"Not yet," Travis said. "I worked a homicide scene until sunup this morning. Just came home to clean up and get a short nap before I head back into Dallas."

Cannon, Travis and Brit took care of introductions.

"If I can be of any help, let me know," Travis offered.

"I appreciate that," the sheriff said. "I'm just cooperating with the HPD myself. Now if you two will excuse us, Brit and I need to talk."

"You can have the porch," Travis said. "Cannon and I can go inside. I need some coffee, anyway."

Cannon hated being shut out of the discussion with the sheriff, but Brit wasn't going to cut him any slack on this. At least he could run a few of his concerns by Travis.

Captain Bradford couldn't do a damn thing about that.

"DID YOU TELL R.J. that there was another death related to the crime in which Melanie Crouch is a suspect?"

"Yep."

"Who's the victim?"

"Clive Austin."

"You must be mistaken. They've ID'd Clive as the man who attacked me, but he's not dead."

"He is now."

"Where did you get your information?"

"From Carla Bradford."

If Garcia was right, it meant that both Rick and the captain had withheld that information from her. Associating with Cannon was costing her the confidence of her boss and her partner. She had to break away from him entirely.

Garcia walked from the post to one of the rockers. Brit continued to stand.

"Did Captain Bradford say where they found Clive's body?"

"No. Don't hold me to any direct quotes, but the gist of it was that the situation had changed. I asked her what happened. She said Clive Austin had been found murdered."

"That's all she said?"

"It was all she said on that subject. She seemed in a hurry to get off the phone so I didn't question her further. Carla Bradford's a professional.

She'll let me know what I need to know when I need to know it."

Apparently that same professional courtesy no longer extended to Brit. She would call Rick the second Garcia left and demand some answers.

"Want to tell me why you didn't give me the straight scoop last night?" Garcia asked.

"I told you exactly what we were doing in that graveyard."

"You didn't mention that you were recovering from an attack and weren't even supposed to be working the case."

"I was feeling much better. And I don't consider checking on a woman running through a cemetery at night an investigation."

"Not exactly the way it seemed to me when I arrived."

"Melanie pulled a gun on me. I reacted the way any police officer would."

He reached down and nonchalantly knocked a black spider off the arm of the rocker. "I'd have felt the same," he admitted. "Reckon Bradford finally came to the same conclusion."

"What makes you think that?"

"That's the real reason she called back a few minutes ago. She wants you to talk to Melanie before she gets lawyered up. Not that I expect her, too. Far as I know, she's dang near broke."

"She wants me to interrogate Melanie?"

"Yep. We'll have to read Melanie her rights since this could lead to her arrest as a suspect in a murder case and not just a parole violator."

"When can I see her?"

"As soon as I get back to Oak Grove. In fact, you can ride into town with me. I'll have one of my deputies give you a lift back to the ranch when you're finished."

"I can be ready in five minutes or less."

"Hold your horses. We're not in that big a hurry. Melanie's not going anywhere. I got some business out this way I need to take care of before we go back into Oak Grove. I'll be back to pick you up in under an hour."

"Perfect." That would give her time to talk to Rick and get the full scoop on where they'd found Clive's body.

Garcia stood and hiked up his khaki trousers. "Bradford did make one stipulation, though. She doesn't want Cannon anywhere near the suspect."

"He won't be."

"Okeydokey. In the meantime, you be careful," Garcia said. "You've had two people try to kill you in two days. As we say around here, you're wallowing in danger."

"I'm a cop. It goes with the job."

BRIT PUNCHED IN Rick's speed dial number on her cell phone.

Rick answered the phone. "Damn, partner. You picked a hell of a time to go running off with a bull rider. You're missing all the excitement."

"Where are you?"

"In a crummy apartment on the southeast side of Houston working a crime scene. What else would I be doing on a beautiful, crisp, perfect-for-fishing morning?"

"Is it true that Clive Austin's body was found?"

"Yeah. I'm here with the body now. Death does not become him."

Killed by her bullet. In self-defense, but that didn't keep a sickening sensation from weighing on her heart like tons of steel. It wasn't the first time she'd shot someone, but it was the first time she'd taken another life.

She'd always known this day would come, but that made it no easier.

"You still there, Brit?" Rick asked.

"Yeah, just trying to get my mind around my first kill."

"Save the angst. Your record is still intact for now. Clive didn't die from your bullet, though he probably would have, given time, since he didn't have sense enough to go to a hospital."

She took a deep breath and exhaled slowly, renewing her equilibrium. "What killed him?"

"His throat was slit."

"Self-inflicted?"

"Seems doubtful," Rick said, "considering there's no weapon on-site. There is a bloodied car outside registered to him, so apparently he managed to drive himself here after the attack. Judging from the condition of the body, I'd place time of death about twenty-four hours ago."

"Who does the apartment belong to?"

"Clive rented it four days ago using an alias he'd used before. There was no furniture except a dirty futon. No food except an open jar of peanut butter, cracker crumbs and a half-eaten candy bar.

"There was, however, beer in a foam cooler and some weed on the floor next to the futon. The heater was humming and roaches were having a party. Clive was the only attendant not having a good time."

"Convenient robbery of an easy, half-dead victim?"

"Doesn't look that way. His wallet, holding two hundred-dollar bills, was still in his pocket."

Her mind rushed ahead as he described how the body had been found.

"If he was a paid assassin, the woman who hired him must have come back and finished him off to keep him from talking," Brit said, breaking in while he was still talking.

"She or *he*," Rick corrected. "Women are definitely not the only ones who hire killers. Either way, it would mean that Clive's killer has now moved into doing their own dirty work. More reason for you not to take the kind of risk you took last night. There are times even the best of cops need backup. Bull riders don't fill that bill."

"Yet one managed to save my life last night."

"A very lucky break. You could have both been killed."

"But the fact that Melanie pulled a gun on me gives even more credence to my hunch that she's the one behind all of this. Of course, I'll have a better handle on that once I've questioned her—if she talks to me. She knows her way around the system. I look for her to clam up until she gets a lawyer."

"In which case, you need to head back to Houston," Rick said. "I suppose rodeo boy is still at your beck and call."

The comment riled her, but it was just Rick's way. She usually gave as good as she got. This time it was different, but there was no way Rick could know they'd kissed and that it was taking all her willpower to fight the swelling attraction.

"I'll call you after I see Melanie and let you know my plans."

"You got it. Stay safe."

"Yeah, you, too. Get back to work."

He had a crime scene to cover. She had a bull rider to catch up with.

CANNON WAS STANDING with Travis, watching several magnificent horses prance around the corral just behind the horse barn. He'd filled Travis in on the barest of details surrounding the attack on Brit and their run-in with Melanie and Sheriff Garcia last night, careful not to give away any information that might be classified.

"Everybody makes enemies in our line of work," Travis said. "And we deal with some real loonies out there so you can't take anything lightly."

"So I'm learning."

One of the horses moved to the edge of the fence. Cannon reached out and ran his fingers through the long mane before giving the animal a good ear scratching.

The sun's warmth beat through his shirt even though the occasional gusts of wind were cold and the temperature was in the high forties.

According to R.J., the weatherman had promised another light freeze tonight. An early winter storm was moving in from the west, bringing snow and hail to parts of the south.

No more than the possibility of a few flakes

was forecast for Dallas. If they got that, the ground wouldn't be cold enough for it to stick. Heavy snowstorms in Dallas were rare, but even a light snow or coating of ice caused havoc on the roads.

"I'm glad we have this chance to talk alone," Travis said. "I figure that you have your issues with R.J. We all did before we moved onto the Dry Gulch."

Cannon had been expecting but still dreading this conversation. He'd expected it to be initiated by R.J., but probably better discussing it with Travis.

"I guess issues are one way of putting it. More to the point, I have no interest in moving back to the Dry Gulch Ranch. R.J. was never a father to me. I've never been a son to him."

"Far as I know, R.J. wasn't a father to anybody," Travis said. "Not much of a husband, either. He was an alcoholic, a gambler and womanizer."

"That seems to size it up," Cannon agreed. "Great DNA we've inherited."

"Could have been a lot worse," Travis said. "R.J. had a tendency to marry well. At least he did with my mother. Adam says the same, so we have that going for us."

"So what's your point?" Cannon said. "Are

you trying to say I owe R.J. something for providing my mother with sperm?"

"Hardly. Forgiving R.J. has been hard going, even worse for Leif, who hated R.J. more on my account than his. But R.J. has heart and he grows on you. And forgiveness has a way of doing as much or more for the forgiver as for the forgiven."

Travis smiled. "Learned that little gem of truth from my wife, Faith. My philosophy never gets much beyond a man's gotta do what a man's gotta do."

And what Cannon had to do didn't involve the Dry Gulch Ranch. Though he couldn't deny that when he'd gone out walking this morning, the ranch had felt more like home than anywhere he could ever remember being.

"I know you love the rodeo and it's been all you needed until now," Travis continued. "But if it turns out you're a father, your life is about to change big-time. Maybe you should at least consider making the Dry Gulch your headquarters. You could hire a nanny to help with Kimmie, but you'd have family who love her around to make sure she's always in the best of hands."

Cannon hated to admit that Travis made sense—for Kimmie's sake. But Cannon had made up his mind long ago. He'd live life on his terms.

"I'm not much of a team player," Cannon admitted. "And the will specifically stipulates I'd have to live here and work the ranch full-time for at least a year."

"True, but R.J. has already bent the hell out of that provision. Leif's an attorney. I'm with the DPD. Crazy thing is we're both cowboys at heart, same as Adam is. You'd have to blast us out to get us to live anywhere but on the Dry Gulch Ranch now."

"Glad it works for you."

"Just saying, give it some thought," Travis said. "What have you got to lose?"

"Having a ranch of my own." And the freedom to do with it exactly as he pleased.

Cannon looked away and saw Brit heading toward them. He couldn't read her facial expression from this distance, but she was walking fast, long strides, shoulders back, head held high. He hoped that was a good sign and that the news hadn't been as bad as she'd feared.

He pushed Travis's suggestions from his mind as urgent matters took hold. The ache to take Brit in his arms and absorb some of her worry and fears hit hard as she approached. But one kiss did not a relationship make, no matter how electrifying it had been.

"How did it go?" he asked.

"I'm actually not sure yet, but you'll be glad

to know that Captain Bradford changed her mind and said it was okay for me to interrogate Melanie Crouch."

"Back in the saddle again," Cannon said. "That is good news."

"Yes it is, but you're still persona non grata as far as Bradford is concerned."

"That figures. Whose body was found?"

"My attacker was found with his throat split. Apparently someone who knew where he was had come back and finished him off."

"When did they find the body?" Cannon asked.

"Within the past hour. My partner had just arrived at the crime scene to verify the ID of the victim. The maintenance manager called 911 when he spotted what looked like blood that had spilled out from under the door. The officers who responded to his 911 call recognized Clive from the APB bulletin put out on him shortly before that."

"Would that by any chance be Clive Austin?" Travis asked.

"Yes. Have you ever heard of him?"

"More than just heard of him. I have a warrant out for his arrest. He's the primary suspect in an armed robbery of a convenience store last month that left a teenage customer badly wounded and a young clerk dead. If you've got a minute, Brit, we need to talk, detective to detective."

"Guess that's my signal to get lost," Cannon said.

"That's up to Brit," Travis said. "Your being here doesn't bother me. We're hanging out at a corral with family, not in a court of law. Besides, the way I see it, you're already involved or you wouldn't have been in that cemetery getting your life threatened last night."

"You've got a point," Brit said, "though my immediate supervisor doesn't seem to see it that way."

"Works by the book, huh?"

"Most of the time."

"Your call, then, but I doubt you're going to tell me anything that Cannon doesn't already know."

"Right again," Brit agreed.

Travis hooked his heels behind the lowest slat in the wooden fence and propped his backside on the top slat. "So fill me in on the pertinent details of your case."

Cannon propped himself on the top slat, as well. Brit stood between them, rehashing everything that had happened since the attack on her life two days ago.

"Did Clive Austin have any reason to hold

a personal grudge against your sister?" Travis asked.

"Not that I know of. I'm sure that's being looked into."

"What about a grudge against your father?"

"Marcus Garner— Again, not that I know of."

"So you're the daughter of Marcus Garner," Travis said. "I've heard of him though never actually met him. He was well-respected in the business."

"And a great man."

"Seems odd that Clive referenced your being like your father if he'd never had dealings with him."

"Dad did a lot to clean up crime in the inner city. That earned him lots of enemies in the criminal population."

"According to Cannon, Melanie Crouch just got out of jail for paying someone to murder her husband," Travis said.

"Yes, Richard Crouch, a very prominent Houston surgeon before he was killed."

"I remember the case," Travis said. "Dr. Crouch was a sleaze."

"Yes, but few people knew that until the trial brought out all his dirty secrets."

"Was the doctor a friend of your father?" Cannon asked, still trying to make sense of this.

"They'd met. I don't know that they were friends."

"That connection could be worth looking into," Travis said. "Did your dad have a long-time good friend, someone he spent a lot of time with? Someone who might know things about him no one else did?"

"Aidan McIntosh. They were in college together and joined the police force about the same time. They were partners for most of the time Dad was in Homicide. He was the best man at my parents' wedding. Their son, Matt, even took me to the senior prom after I broke up with my boyfriend the day before. Of course, we had no idea then that Aidan and Louise's son was already dealing crack cocaine."

"Where is Matt McIntosh now?" Cannon asked.

"In prison for killing two completely innocent people in a drive-by execution. The worst part of all was that Aidan had tried to cover for him before that. But once his son committed murder, he realized he couldn't protect him any longer. He agreed to testify against his son and turn himself in, but only to my father. I think the worst day of Dad's life was when he had to arrest his best friend."

"Is Aidan still in prison?" Travis asked.

"No, he was released four years ago, a year

before my father was murdered. He and his wife live in Plano now. He works as a night security manager for one of the shopping malls."

"Might be a good idea to pay him a visit," Travis suggested."

Brit shook her head. "Aidan had nothing to do with the attack on me. I'd stake my life on that."

"But in case Melanie isn't the culprit, Aidan might have insight into who may have paid Clive to do it, especially if the attack on you was connected to your father."

"It's not far to Plano," Cannon said. "We could drive up there this afternoon after you finish questioning Melanie."

"If you do, get back here early," Travis cautioned. "A little ice on the road in Dallas and fender benders pop up at every intersection."

"We won't be coming back to the ranch tonight," Brit said. "If I'd been thinking clearly, I wouldn't have stayed last night. I will not bring danger onto the Dry Gulch Ranch and I'm afraid my being here is doing just that."

The decision surprised Cannon. She downplayed danger to herself so well that he'd feared she wasn't taking it seriously. He should have known better. Determined enough to do what it took solve the case. Brave enough she'd do whatever it took to bring a killer down—unless the killer got her first.

He had no intention of letting that happen.

"I guess the good news is that if Melanie is the person who paid Clive Austin to kill me and Sylvie, she was most likely taken to jail before she could find someone else to take over for him."

"But we have no proof that Melanie hired him, so your life is still very much in danger," Travis cautioned. "What I can't make sense of is how Melanie would know that Sylvie was your sister when you didn't even know it."

"Maybe she didn't know," Cannon suggested. "At least not when Sylvie was still alive. You and Sylvie looked so much alike that Clive could have killed her believing she was you."

"She was in the vicinity of my office when she was killed," Brit said. "And near the coffee shop that I frequent every morning."

"If that's the case, Melanie Crouch makes a strong suspect," Travis said.

"It gives me a new angle to look at," Brit said. "I have to go back to the house now. Sheriff Garcia should be back to pick me up any minute and I want to say goodbye to Kimmie before I go into Oak Grove with him."

"You know you don't have to stay away tonight," Travis said. "The Daltons stick together. And we easily have enough men and wranglers to protect you."

"I can protect myself, but I refuse to put others at risk."

"Then take this." Travis reached into his pocket and pulled out a key ring. He slipped one small silver key from the ring and handed it to Cannon. "This is to my condo in Dallas. I keep it for the nights I can't make it home at all. Gives me a place to grab a shower and a nap."

Travis took a card and pen from his pocket, scribbled down an address and handed that to Cannon, as well. "Call if you need anything, and, Brit, keep me posted. I want to hear how that chat with Melanie Crouch comes out."

They said their goodbyes. Travis lingered at the corral. Cannon took Brit's hand as they walked back to the ranch house together. His need for her was as much about making sure she stayed alive as it was about the physical side of things.

Still, how in the world would he spend the night alone with her in Travis's town house without sleeping with her?

The answer was simple. He couldn't without going nuts.

Chapter Fourteen

Fury raged inside her, all but crippling her ability to think clearly. Everything had been planned down to the most insignificant detail. There was no reason for anything to go wrong.

And yet it had.

Clive Austin was dead. Brit Garner was alive.

But not for long.

That wouldn't give her back the joy and anticipation she'd enjoyed once, but it would make life bearable. Perhaps she'd even be able to sleep again without the terrifying nightmares.

At one time all her life had stretched out in front of her like a field of wildflowers ready to burst into bloom. She had been young and pretty and excited about life.

And then life had crashed down on her, wave after wave of fear and insufferable heartache.

The only thing she had to hold on to was revenge. It burned inside her, gave her a reason to live.

That's why Brit had to die.

Clive Austin had screwed up the perfect plan, but that was only a detour. The perfect ending was coming.

The plans were in motion even now. And this time nothing could stop them—not Cannon Dalton, not the Houston Police Department and not Detective Brit Garner.

She might spend the rest of her life in prison, but what did it matter? Her life was devastated beyond salvation. Everything that mattered to her was lost.

Someone had to pay for destruction like that.

Chapter Fifteen

Brit felt Melanie's fury the second she stepped into the small interrogation room. The anger hung thick in the air and seemed to drip from the glaring ceiling light above the table that separated them like a tangible entity.

But the woman sitting across the table from Brit was not the ghostly, barefoot nymph who'd haunted the cemetery last night. Today her hair was neatly brushed and she looked totally in control.

Garcia had decided to watch the meeting from behind the one-way glass—nearby in case Melanie became violent, yet out of sight as Brit had requested.

Brit had her own way of questioning, a blend of what she'd learned from her father and her own experience. Some detectives pushed and shoved and browbeat a suspect down until they cracked under pressure.

Brit couldn't have pulled that off if she'd

wanted to. She fit more into the good-cop mold. She let her suspects talk freely, pretended to identify with their plight.

Feeling they were winning, the guilty tended to hammer their own points home, defend even the most indefensible behaviors, justify until they ended up providing the very information that would lead to conviction.

But Melanie already hated Brit so she'd be coming into this ready for a fight.

Melanie looked straight at Brit, her eyes shooting daggers. "So nice of you to come by and chat this morning, Detective."

"I am just here to talk, Melanie. I'm sorry we got off to such a bad start last night, but sarcasm isn't going to help."

"Sorry. I must have forgotten my manners. Prison does that to a lady. So let's get down to business. Exactly what crime are you trying to pin on me this time?"

"You mean other than you pulling a gun on me last night and threatening to kill me?"

"You were stalking me in the dark, behind my own house. I feared for my life."

"I wasn't stalking you. I simply checked to see if a woman roaming around a cemetery at night was in trouble."

"You were there because you know I should keep my word and come after you. You turned that jury against me with all your talk of my options. Well, let me set the record straight, Detective. When you live with a man as rich and powerful as Richard Crouch, there are no options."

"You mean no options that wouldn't leave you broke."

"You have no idea what it was like married to a man like Richard. Cross him in any way and you pay. Verbal abuse. Psychological abuse. Mental abuse. There's no end to the ways he could torment you."

All of which Melanie had detailed to the jury from the stand.

"You're right, Melanie. I can only imagine what he put you through. Flaunting the fact that he was involved with a much younger woman. Knowing it was only a matter of time before he divorced you. A lot of women would break under that kind of pressure."

"There were always other women."

"He must have promised that would never happen again when he left his second wife for you."

"Lies. Every word out of his mouth was a lie. He twisted things around, put words in my mouth, just the way you do, Detective. He deserved to die." Her voice rose with rage, but the venom in her eyes suggested the fury was directed at Brit and not her murdered husband.

"I didn't convict you, Melanie. All I did was give the evidence to the prosecution. I had nothing to do with the trial."

"You had everything to do with it. Your testimony was the one that swayed the jury. I had them in my hands before that. They believed my desperation, understood that Richard had made me an emotional prisoner. They would have known I needed counseling, not a prison sentence."

"If you really feel that way, I can see why you wanted me dead."

"I wanted you dead all right. More than anything in the world I wanted to see you dead. I lay awake night after night thinking of how I'd kill you when I was free."

"I'm sorry you felt that way. I was only doing my job. I can't believe you wanted me dead so badly that you're willing to go back to prison."

"I don't. And that's the only reason you're still alive, Brit Garner. I would rather die than live behind bars. So stay away from me. I paid my debt to this hypocritical society and I'm moving on, leaving you and Texas and every memory of Richard far behind."

"Is that what you told Clive Austin before you killed him?"

Melanie's muscles visibly tensed, the veins in her neck and forehead cording and turning a vivid blue. "I don't know what you're talking about. I don't know a Clive Austin."

"I think you do, Melanie, and it would go much better for you if you tell the truth. Were you in Houston this week?"

Melanie jumped from her chair and repeatedly beat her fist against the table. "I know what you're doing, Detective. I want a lawyer. I'm not saying another word until I get one."

Garcia stepped back into the room. "That's enough, Melanie. You can hire a lawyer, but the only charge against you right now is for breaking your probation by carrying a firearm. If you have anything else to confess, you'd be wise to do it now and hope for leniency."

"Go to hell, both of you. And when you get there, Brit, say hello to Richard for me."

CANNON STOPPED IN front of the old cemetery where they'd encountered Melanie last night. It looked more deteriorated than spooky in the bright light of day.

Not that he'd been scared of ghosts since the Halloween he was five and one had jumped out at him from behind a tree. Even then, he'd kicked the older kid in the shins before he'd run away.

Actually, he'd never been afraid of much in his life, though he had a healthy respect for what a bull could do to a body given half a chance.

But he'd had a crash course in fear the past few days. One truth he'd learned firsthand was that it didn't always come from the outside. Some of it spewed up straight from the gut.

Like the fear of becoming a father when you had no idea how to begin and no time to prepare. The anxiety wasn't just about him but also for Kimmie.

Talk about getting a raw deal from the get-go. The infant's mother had been murdered. Her father might turn out to the worst choice of dad ever. Well, the second-worst candidate. Surely R.J. would top the list.

But the most pressing terror centered on Brit. It bucked around inside Cannon with such force that he hated having her out of his sight for a second. Even now, when he knew she was with Sheriff Garcia, he worried.

All it took was one second of opportunity to slit someone's throat, the way someone had killed Clive. The way someone had attempted to kill Brit.

The fact that she was a trained police officer and insisted she could protect herself did little to lessen his apprehension. He'd been going crazy uselessly sitting around the Dry Gulch. That's why he'd driven out to the cemetery. He figured the police had already acted on information from Brit and checked out the freshly dug mound of dirt, but he might as well make sure.

This time instead of walking around the church, he walked through it, sidestepping broken hunks of concrete and a chunk of the decaying outer walls. The roof was completely gone. The lonely spire was all that was left to beckon visitors to a deserted graveyard.

He stooped to pick up a small broken piece of pottery. He had no idea what it had been, but the remaining shape would work for scooping up loose dirt.

Not as good as a shovel, but it would do. He slipped it into his pocket and made his way to the overgrown graveyard.

It took him ten minutes to find the freshly dug plot in the maze of cracked and crumbling headstones and aged monuments. He kicked most of the dirt away with the heel of his boot then stooped over and scooped until he reached what he thought was a small box.

When his fingers felt the edges, he realized it wasn't a box but a large book. He freed it from the mound and brushed off the remaining dirt with his hand. He was holding a photograph album.

Odd that Melanie Crouch would come to a

deserted graveyard at night to bury pictures— unless they were more of the sickening photos Clive Austin had taken of Sylvie after he'd stabbed and killed her.

Cannon opened the book and skimmed the pages. It was a wedding album.

He recognized the bride at once, though Melanie was years younger. By anyone's standards, she'd been beautiful. Young. Shapely.

The bridal gown looked like one of those extravagant concoctions that you saw on the covers of gossip magazines. But the necklace was the real showstopper. A man cold buy a small plane for what that must have cost.

The marriage between Melanie and Richard Crouch had had obviously started off with a bang. It had ended with his murder by the bride looking at him in the picture like he was Greek god that had sprung to life in Armani clothing.

"Police. Put your hands over your head. Try anything funny and you can have your own grave."

Cannon did as ordered. The album fell to the ground, bounced off the pottery chunk and landed facedown. He spun around and looked into the barrel of a .45.

"Stand still and keep your hands above your head."

The man giving the order had a deputy sheriff

patch sewed onto the arm of his khaki shirt. He stooped down and picked up the album.

"This is a wedding album," the deputy said, as if this were some kind of joke. "You're robbing graves for someone else's wedding pictures. What kind of freak are you?"

"I didn't rob a grave. I just unearthed the album from that mound of dirt."

"Are you the one who buried it there?"

"No. I'm Cannon Dalton. I was here with Detective Brittany Garner from the Houston Police Department last night and we spotted the fresh-dug mound."

"And you came back to dig it up?"

"Right. I thought it might contain evidence in a murder case. This is a complicated story."

"I'll bet."

"You can call Sheriff Garcia now. He'll verify what I'm saying."

"You got some ID on you?"

"If you'll let me get my wallet without shooting me."

"Let's see it." He finally retuned his automatic to his holster.

Cannon showed him his Texas driver's license. The deputy took only a second to check it out.

"You must be R.J.'s son—the bull rider."

Cannon nodded.

"I saw you ride once at the Dallas Rodeo. You won first place and you stayed on a bone-buster of a bull to do it."

"Thanks." So now they were old friends. Cannon looked around. "How did you get out here, anyway? I don't see a vehicle."

The deputy spit a stream of brown tobacco into the grass. "My horse is tethered over at the old Stanton spread. I live down the road so decided to ride over when the sheriff asked me to keep an eye on the house today.

"I saw you poking through the church and the graveyard and figured you were up to no good. It was quiet, but you still would have heard me if you hadn't been so engrossed in that album."

"Probably so."

"You say you were here with a Houston detective last night."

"That's right."

"That album wouldn't have anything to do with Melanie Crouch, would it? You know she was a Stanton before she married that rich Houston doctor."

"Did you know her when she was Melanie Stanton?"

"Nope. Her parents were both dead and she was long gone before I moved to Oak Grove. My wife and I bought a little land and built us a house out here after she retired from teaching school. Got tired of city life."

"Then you haven't seen Melanie since she got out of prison?"

"I've seen her coming and going. That's it. Just as well. Didn't take her long to get back into trouble."

"Did you hear that from the sheriff?"

"No, but I'm supposed to keep everyone away from the house until he can get a search warrant to go in and look for evidence. That spells trouble to me."

"Guess it does.

"If you're going to call the sheriff, I'd appreciate your doing it now," Cannon said. "I need to get back to town. In fact, I can take the album to him."

"That's okay. You can go anytime, but I think I'd best hold on to the album and give it to Sheriff Garcia myself."

"Whatever you think best."

Cannon had done what he came for, verified that Melanie had not been out there to bury evidence last night but her wedding pictures. He understood the act considering how the marriage turned out.

But that still left them with no solid evidence against Melanie Crouch. Clive Austin might be dead, but the world was full of lowlifes who'd do anything for a buck—even murder.

Cannon's phone rang. He checked the caller ID. It was Brit.

"All finished here," Brit said. "If you still want to drive to Plano, you can pick me up at the sheriff's office in Oak Grove."

"Works for me. How did the interrogation go?"

"Well enough that I still think Melanie Crouch is a very strong suspect. I'll fill you in when I see you."

"I'm on my way." And he was not letting Brit out of his sight again until he was sure she was safe.

But she'd never really be out of danger. She was a cop. She'd walk right back into danger again. And again. And again.

"YOU'LL NEED THIS," Cannon said. He held Brit's jacket for her as she slipped into it. Then he reached to the backseat and grabbed the sandwiches they'd bought at an Oak Grove coffee shop. Brit could have skipped lunch, but Cannon had insisted on food.

They'd decided to get the sandwiches to go. The place was entirely too crowded and noisy for private conversation. A small park two blocks from the sheriff's office seemed ideal.

They trekked up a slight incline and chose a picnic table in the shade of a giant oak. The only other people in the park were a young mother and her two children and they were yards away playing on a bright red tubular slide.

"Turkey-and-avocado wrap. This has to be yours," Cannon said as he pulled out her wrapped sandwich and handed it to her. "Real men eat real sandwiches."

Brit took one look at his oversize sub and shuddered. "You won't even be able to get your mouth around that."

"Watch me."

He took a huge bite out of the sandwich, proving her wrong. She lifted their covered cups of hot coffee from the bag and set them on the table next to them.

Cannon delved into the rest of his sandwich like a starving man. She enjoyed watching him eat. Not that there was a lot about Cannon she didn't like. A definite contrast to the way she'd felt about him before they'd met.

That had only been three days ago and yet she felt more attached to him than anyone she knew. It wasn't just the kiss or the way he made her senses strum with awareness. It was the way he'd looked holding Kimmie this morning—nervous, awkward, fatherly. The way he'd come to her rescue at the hospital with no questions asked.

The way he'd gone tramping through a dark graveyard with her. The way he'd saved her life.

"I'm all but convinced Melanie is the one who paid Clive to kill me and then killed him when he failed," she said, determined to get her mind off her growing attraction for Cannon.

"So you said when I picked you up. How about some details?"

Brit went over Melanie's response to the questions and then described her reactions when the subject of Clive Austin came up.

"She claimed she'd never heard of him, but her actions and facial expressions said differently. And when I asked her about being in Houston, she demanded a lawyer. It's not the solid evidence we'll need to hold her in jail, but hopefully we'll have that soon. Sheriff Garcia has already requested a warrant to search that old house she's staying in."

"I heard."

"From whom?"

"A very interesting tobacco-chewing deputy who caught me digging up our mysterious mound in the graveyard."

"When were you there?"

"When you called me to come and pick you up."

"You are a constant surprise, Cannon Dalton. You should think about becoming a detective."

"No, I'll take mad bulls over crazy criminals any day."

She listened as he told about finding the buried wedding album.

"Not the evidence I was hoping for," Brit admitted, "but it is very interesting."

Cannon sipped his coffee. "Seems like a lot of trouble to go to when she could have just tossed it in the trash."

"But burying is more symbolic," Brit said. "It gives closure, a way of putting that part of your life behind you forever."

"I'd say the closure part is not working if Melanie's still out to kill you."

"It does seem a bit odd when you think of it like that, but no one has ever accused Melanie of being rational."

"How much evidence do you need to keep her in jail with no chance of bail?"

"A murder weapon. An explicit connection to Clive. An eye witness. A confession. Any of those would go a long way."

"They don't make this easy, do they?"

"Innocent until proven guilty." Brit dropped the remainder of her sandwich into the empty bag along with both their napkins. "Let's not talk about Melanie or Clive or my attack for the next five minutes. I only want pleasant conversation and a walk down that bike trail that cuts through the trees while I finish my coffee."

"Okay." Cannon stood and tugged her to a standing position. "You pick the topic."

"Let's talk about you."

"Where shall we start?"

Brit dropped their trash into a nearby container as they started toward the trail. "How about when you were a kid?"

"I thought you wanted pleasant."

"Did you have a terrible childhood?"

"Not in the beginning."

"Then let's start there. How old were you when you left the Dry Gulch Ranch?"

"I'm not sure I ever made it to the Dry Gulch, at least not once I was out of my mother's womb."

"Your mother divorced R.J. that quickly."

"That's the way she tells it."

"What happened?"

"She went into labor early. R.J. was off on a drunk and no one could find him. She decided that she didn't want to be married to an alcoholic so she called an attorney from the hospital and started divorce proceedings. At least, that's the way she told it. And if you'd ever met my mother, you'd know she was impulsive enough to do just that."

"That must have been terrible for her. A single parent with a new baby."

"Looking back, I'm sure she didn't let it get her down. My mother was the most upbeat, outgoing, optimistic woman I've ever met. Our house was always full of friends. Men and women. Mom loved music and dancing and had boundless energy. The other kids always liked to hang out at my house to just to be around her."

"Who wouldn't?"

"Did I mention that she was also good-looking—kind of a young Meg Ryan only her hair was red instead of blond. I didn't realize how cute she was at the time, of course. She was just Mom then. Luckily I have pictures of the two of us together going back to the time I was a baby."

"What great memories."

"It was all good—until it ended."

"What happened?"

"She went water-skiing one weekend with a group of friends. Someone in a speedboat slammed into them when she was getting back in the boat. She was crushed in the mangled wreckage. She died in the ambulance on the way to the E.R."

"Oh, Cannon. How sad. You must have missed her terribly."

"I did. I didn't seem to fit in the world without her. I went home from the funeral with my mother's brother. I don't think he ever liked me. I know I never liked him, but you do what you're told when you're thirteen."

"Someone should have called R.J. and let him know," Brit said.

"My uncle called him and asked him for money for my support. R.J. told him he didn't consider me a son, said he doubted I was even his."

"Surely not."

"I told you this was ugly. Heard enough?"

"Enough that I understand why you have no use for R.J. But something must have changed his mind about you. He seems glad to see you now and he included you in his will."

"Too little. Too late. I'm not interested in his money or his ranch. I had enough of being bossed around by my uncle. I'll have enough money in a few years to buy my own ranch and run it exactly as I please. At least that's the way I had it planned before…"

He didn't finish the sentence, but she knew what he was thinking. Finding out he was a father would wreck those plans. Had Sylvie known that? Was that why she'd decided not to tell him about Kimmie?

Only how well could Sylvie have known Cannon after only one night?

But they had made love even if Cannon

didn't remember it. He'd kissed Brit once and pulled away.

"I guess we should get started back to the truck if we want to catch Aidan and his wife before dinner time."

"I think so."

Only he didn't start walking. He trailed a finger up her arm and then tucked his thumb beneath Brit's chin. Her head was spinning as he tilted her head so that she couldn't avoid meeting his gaze and staring into the deep depths of his brown eyes.

Brit felt giddy, suddenly weak. Cannon kissed her forehead, her eyelids—the tip of her nose. Her heart pounded in her chest.

And then his lips met hers and explosions of desire ripped through her body. His fingers tangled in her hair and he pulled her closer. She arched toward him, so lost in the kiss that all she wanted was more of him.

He came up for air, only to trail his lips from her mouth to her earlobe. "I've wanted to do that all day," he whispered. "You are driving me crazy without even trying."

"Crazy can be good."

He slipped his hands beneath the back of her shirt and his fingers danced along her bare skin. She found his lips again and melted into the thrill of him. No one had ever made her feel desirable. No one had ever made every area of her body ache for more of him.

Her phone rang. Her first impulse was to ignore it. But realty pushed through the passion.

"I have to," she said, pulling away.

"Brit, this is Sheriff Garcia. You called it and got it all right."

Chapter Sixteen

Cannon kept his eyes on the interstate, but listened intently, trying to keep up with Brit's analysis of the sheriff's findings. She was ecstatic, talking fast and throwing in so much police lingo he was having difficulty following her.

"How about slowing down and speaking in English?"

"Sorry. Most important development is that Melanie's arrest is imminent."

"I got that part. I'm lost somewhere in the midst of graveyard timing, phone records, new clothes, fuel tank and opportunity."

"Elementary and evidential, babe. Luck and good police work, the two most important weapons in a detective's arsenal."

"Not to mention my Smith & Wesson that came to the party last night."

"That goes without saying. Did I ever thank you for saving my life?"

"Not appropriately," he teased. Or maybe he

wasn't teasing. He'd never wanted a woman more—nor been more certain he was heading for heartbreak.

"I could bake you a cake," she teased right back. "Well, actually, I can't cook, but I could buy one from the bakery."

"I'm not that into cake."

"Back to the timing," she quipped, wisely changing the subject before they started something they couldn't stop and risked never making it to Plano.

Brit kicked out of one black pump and pulled her bare foot into the seat with her. She shifted, so that she was facing him. "You played a major part in the timing, without which we wouldn't have hit the evidence jackpot or have a case against Melanie."

"All I did was drive and follow your orders."

"Requests, not orders," Brit reminded him, excitement still singing in her voice. "Fifteen minutes earlier or later and we would have missed seeing Melanie in the cemetery. She wouldn't have pulled a gun on me. There would have been no arrest for breaking the rules of her parole.

"Melanie was carted off to jail so unexpectedly she didn't have time to dispose of evidence. Her handbag and phone were on her bed in plain sight when they searched her house, as were two packed suitcases."

"Did it look as if she were returning from somewhere or leaving?"

"Definitely leaving, most likely permanently. There was nothing left in the drawers of her chest or her dresser. Her luggage was packed with an all-new wardrobe. Most of the clothes still had the tags on them. Most of it beachwear."

"Off to a Caribbean Island or perhaps Mexico," Cannon said, thinking out loud.

"Definitely somewhere warm," Brit agreed. "If we hadn't driven here last night, Melanie and her evidence might have been long gone before she was questioned."

"Not following orders paid off that time," Cannon said.

"Which should put me back in good standing with Captain Bradford."

"Did they find any plane tickets?"

"No, but you can always buy those at the last minute, a common practice of people unlawfully fleeing the country."

"Did she have the requisite fake passport?"

"None was found. But she could have been flying out on a private jet or picking a fake passport up on her way to the airport. I'm sure she wouldn't have any trouble making those arrangements. After almost five years in prison, Melanie surely knows people in low places."

"Will you be able to get a transcript of the phone calls between Brit and Clive?"

"No, but we have the date and times the calls were made, whether they were incoming or outgoing and the lengths of the calls."

"And Clive Austin's name actually came up on the phone records?"

"Yes, but we're talking about the records on the phone itself. It was a prepaid phone, the kind you can buy at any convenience store. She probably planned on destroying it before she fled the area."

"When were the calls made?"

"They talked twice two days before my attack, both calls short and initiated by Clive."

"That doesn't quite add up if Melanie was the one looking to hire him."

"The first contact with him was likely made in person through a trusted third party."

"That makes sense," Cannon said. "I doubt a killer for hire would be advertising. How many other phone contacts were there between the two of them?"

"Only one," Brit said. "She called him the morning of my attack. The phone call lasted ten minutes, plenty of time to go over last-minute details like the location of the apartment where he was found dead. She may have arranged to deliver the final payment there, if all had gone well."

"Sounds like a lot of supposition."

"That's not unusual in murder cases, unless you have an eye witness. But the supposition is based on facts. What the sheriff uncovered provides solid evidence that Melanie was lying when she said she didn't know Clive and that there was communication between them just prior to Clive's failed attempt on my life and his murder."

"You mentioned discovering a key to a safety deposit box in her handbag when you were speed talking. How does that fit into the evidence framework?"

"There's no direct link at this point, but it does indicate she had something of value. It was always suspected that she had made off with some gold bars and a few very expensive pieces of jewelry that were never accounted for after Richard Crouch's murder. Selling them on the black market would explain where she got the money to hire Clive and pay for her stylish new wardrobe, and leave enough for her to live on once she'd settled in paradise."

"Must have been a chunk of shiny rocks to bring in that kind of dough."

"Her late husband was a very rich man."

"Any idea who fenced the gold and jewelry?"

"No, but they found a receipt for a full tank of gas purchased at an Oak Grove service station four days ago. Her tank is almost empty now. She'd have never used that much gas just driving into Oak Grove and back."

"So we have motive, ability and opportunity," Cannon said. "Gotta hand it to Sheriff Garcia. That was a nice day's work."

"Agreed. He's a far shrewder investigator than I would have guessed from our cemetery meeting."

"So what happens next?" Cannon asked.

"Melanie will be arrested for paying someone to murder Sylvie, Clive and me, even though I survived. Those charges will insure she won't qualify for bail."

Brit reached over and laid a hand on his thigh. The slight touch set off a spiral of arousal. It was downright scary that a simple touch from her could have that strong an effect on him. Not only did it turn him on physically, but also it felt familiar, as if her hand belonged there, and that touched him on a dozen other levels.

"Seriously, I can't thank you enough for the part you played in all of this, Cannon. I'm not sure why you ended up at the hospital the morning after my attack, but I'm sure glad you did."

"I'm not sure why I did, either," he said truthfully. "Guess it was meant to be."

"I like that sentiment."

"Do you still want to go to Plano?"

"I would—if you don't mind. I'd like hear what Aidan McIntosh thinks about the case against Melanie. Most of all, it would give me a chance to ask him if he knows anything about my adoption."

"Good thinking."

Brit's mood lightened dramatically as they drove the last few miles toward Plano. He'd barely been able to resist Brit when she'd been obsessed with finding Sylvie's killer and her attacker. Now she was completely intoxicating.

His phone rang as they exited the freeway in Plano. "R.J.," he said, willing to let the call go unanswered.

"You have to answer it," Brit urged. "It could concern Kimmie."

Reluctantly, Cannon took the call and switched to speaker so Brit could listen in on the conversation.

"I hear you two swooped in and showed Garcia how to solve a murder case in record time," R.J. said.

"Brit and the sheriff did the work. I just hung around and watched."

"That's not how Garcia is telling it. He's ready to hire you on the spot."

"Tell him I appreciate the offer, but I'll stick to bull riding."

"Travis said you two were going to stay in town tonight because Brit didn't want to bring any trouble our way. Never was any need for that but sure as shootin' ain't no reason for that now. Adam and Leif are grilling Dry Gulch steaks tonight. No trouble to add two more."

"Don't count on us for dinner. We're in Plano right now and I'm not sure how long we'll be."

"What in Sam Hill are you doing way up there?"

"Taking care of some personal business." He wasn't about to start explaining his comings and goings to R.J.

"Even if you get here late, would be nice to have you. Tomorrow's Saturday and the whole family will be around. Be a good chance for you and Brit to get to know everyone. If Kimmie's your daughter, Brit will be part of the family, too."

As if that were an honor. "No use to rush things."

"No use to make things harder than they have to be, either, Cannon. Up to you, but Leif's daughter, Effie, and Faith's son, Cornell, have big plans for the morning. They're calling it our first ever annual Christmas Tree Search. Everyone will be splitting up into teams and going out on horseback to see who can find the most perfect Christmas tree. My neighbor Mattie Mae is coming over for the fun. She'll be here to watch Kimmie."

"I doubt we can make it."

"You do what you think's best, but you'll be missed."

Brit barely waited until the connection was broken to light into him.

"Did you have to be that rude? They're taking care of your daughter."

"*Possibly* my daughter. And I appreciate that, but I'm not going to play the happy-family game when I have no intention of making R.J. part of my life."

"He's your father and he's reaching out to you. Would it hurt you to at least give him a chance? It's not as if he'll be around forever."

"He was never around, not for me. Wouldn't even admit I was his son."

"He's admitting it now. At least talk to him. Tell him how you feel and why. It might be good for both of you to get things out in the open."

"I just can't see the point of it."

"Have it your way, but I want to go back to the Dry Gulch tonight."

Now he'd ticked her off—the last thing he'd wanted to do. "Afraid to stay alone with me at

Travis's condo?" he teased, hoping to get her back in a good mood.

"Not afraid in the least," she said. "Didn't you hear R.J.? I'm part of the family, and I don't want to miss the first ever annual Christmas Tree Search."

AIDAN MCINTOSH POURED a double shot of Scotch into a glass while he waited for Brit's arrival.

He figured the talk tonight would concern Sylvie, since he'd only had one short conversation with Brit since her sister's death. Marcus had always hoped that Sylvie and Brit would meet someday when the time was right. Aidan didn't see the time as ever being right.

Brit's father had always been a hero in Brittany's eyes, bigger than life, more an idol to her than any movie or sports star.

Aidan didn't have the heart or the right to soil Marcus's memory.

He took his drink to the family room. His wife joined him there seconds later. "You should have told Brit we were busy."

"We're not busy."

Her hands flew to her narrow hips. Too narrow, to his way of thinking. She was so thin she could have hidden behind a two-by-four.

"Don't go all pious on me, Aidan McIntosh. It's not as if you haven't lied to her before. 'Anything to help out a friend.' Well, look where that got you. Look where it got our son."

Aidan was used to her bitterness and endless nagging about his shortcomings and how he'd failed his family. Through the years he'd learned to shut her out like static on an old radio. Tonight every word from her mouth seared into his conscience.

"You don't owe her anything, Aidan. You definitely wouldn't owe her father as much as a damn if he called from hell."

"Don't start again, Louise. It's not Marcus's fault our son is in prison. Matt made the decisions that ruined his life. He fired the gun that killed innocent people."

"Matt didn't mean to kill the innocent victims. You know that. My Matt is not a killer."

"You've been going over and over this for years, Louise. Please, just give it up."

"How can you give it up, Aidan McIntosh? Marcus Garner ruined your life, and you were his best friend."

"Marcus did the same as I'd have done in his shoes, the same as any honest cop would have done. I broke the law by covering up for Matt's drug dealing. I had to pay the price."

"Still making excuses for Marcus after all these years. Your son and your career were everything to you. Marcus stripped that from you as callously as if you were a stranger he'd passed on the street."

"I took them from myself, Louise."

He'd been too busy enforcing the law to pay attention to what was going on under his own roof. Had he been tuned in to it, he'd have realized that Louise was covering for Matt and his growing drug habit.

The addiction. The dealing. And finally the drive-by shooting that had left a teenager and an innocent child dead and another wounded.

"It's time to tell Brittany the truth about her father, Aidan. She's a big girl now. She can handle it. Marcus doesn't deserve your protection and neither does she."

"Let it go, Louise. We've been over this a hundred times. For God's sake, just let it go."

"No. Not this time. Either you tell her about her so-called adoption or I do."

The doorbell rang.

"I mean it, Aidan. You tell Brittany or I will. Marcus shattered our lives. He stole the one person I loved more than life itself while protecting his own daughter from even a hint of his sins."

"Marcus is dead, Louise. He has been for three years now. Let it go. You can't hurt him. Instead, you're destroying yourself. But if it will help you move past this hatred, I'll tell Brittany everything."

The doorbell rang again. "I'll get it," she said, walking away and smiling as if she'd won some nefarious game. It was the first time he'd seen her smile in years.

BRIT EXCHANGED A warm hug with Aidan. Louise, as always, was more aloof. Louise's affection for Brit had died when her son had been sentenced to life in prison.

At nineteen, Brit hadn't fully understood her pain. After years of seeing the effect of death on so many, she understood it all too well now.

"It's good to see you again, Louise."

"It's been a while. What brings you here tonight?" Louise asked, avoiding any indication that she was glad to see Brit.

"We were in the area and I wanted to drop by and say hello. I hope we didn't pick an inconvenient time."

"Not at all," Aidan said.

"Good. I'd like you to meet a friend of mine." She did the introductions.

Aidan shook Cannon's hand. "Glad to meet any friend of Brit's. Are you with the HPD, too?"

"Afraid not," Cannon said.

"He's a professional bull rider," Brit said. She'd love to add that he was the father of Sylvie's son, but she couldn't very well make that assertion when Cannon wasn't convinced yet.

"Bull riding's tough business," Aidan said. "And the rodeo doesn't sound like city-born-and-bred Brittany's choice of entertainment. How did you two meet?"

"Just good luck on my part," Cannon said.

"Suffice it to say a bull did not bring us together," Brit added, trying to decide how to segue away from small talk to the real reason she was here.

Louise reached into her pocket and pulled out her cell phone. "A text," she said. "I'm sorry. A minor emergency has come up that I need to take care of. I really must go, but I'm sure Aidan can entertain you."

Again the timing couldn't have been better, Brit decided, though she doubted there was really an emergency that had pulled Louise away.

"Can I get you a drink?" Aidan asked as soon as Louise had left the room. "I'm having Scotch on the rocks, but I have most anything you'd like. Bourbon? Vodka?"

"A glass of white wine if you have a bottle open," Brit said. "Otherwise water would be fine."

"How about a Riesling?"

"Perfect."

"That was always your mother's favorite wine."

Cannon asked for beer.

"You two take a seat and make yourselves comfortable. I'll get the drinks and join you in a minute."

"I'd say Louise is less than thrilled to see us, or is she always like that?" Cannon whispered once Aidan was out of earshot.

"She's been less than thrilled to see me ever since my father arrested her son for the murders that sent him to prison for life."

"Guess that could put a damper on a friendship. I get the feeling she and Aidan aren't on the best of terms tonight, either. We may have interrupted a family squabble."

"Possibly. We won't stay long."

"Probably a good idea, anyway, if you still want to drive back to the Dry Gulch tonight. We're already going to catch Friday-night traffic."

Aidan returned with their drinks. Brit and Cannon had settled on the nutmeg-colored sofa. Aidan paced. He was definitely upset about something.

"Have you made any progress in apprehending Sylvie Hamm's killer?" he asked.

Brit couldn't have hoped for a better opening. "We're making progress. I can't discuss the case yet, but I think we may have her killer in jail."

"That is good news."

"Yes, I wish I could say the same about Dad's

killer, but I'm still getting nowhere with that. It's incredibly frustrating."

"I'm sure it is, but you'll get there one day, probably when you least expect it."

"I hope you're right. Actually, we came here tonight because I have a few questions that I hope you can answer."

"Shoot."

"I know how close you and my dad were, right from college on. He must have shared a lot of things with you."

"Some."

"Did he ever mention that I had a twin sister?"

Aidan drank the last half of his Scotch in one gulp. "He did. I've kept those secrets for thirty years, but I guess it's time you know the truth."

Chapter Seventeen

"I know that he was my father in every way that mattered. No one could ever take his place, but I'd like to know more about the adoption. Mainly I'd like to know why Sylvie and I were separated at birth and why I was never told I had a twin."

"Marcus was your biological father, Brit. You need to know that before you can understand the rest of the story."

The statement caught her off guard. Aidan had seemed so serious, but surely he was joking. Only he didn't look like he was joking.

Aidan buried his head in his hands for long seconds before he looked up again and met Brit's steady gaze. "Sylvie's mother and Marcus were lovers. You and Sylvie were born of that love."

Brit swallowed hard, unwilling to believe Aidan's words. "You must be mistaken. My dad loved my mother. He never even looked at another woman. Everyone who knew him said that."

"And they'd be right, except for a woman named Gabriel Hamm. He fell for her the second he met her."

"Are you sure?" Brit tried but couldn't keep the tremble from her voice.

"I'm sure," Aidan said. "I was there the night they met."

"Was it a one-night stand?" Someone her father had hooked up with the way Cannon had hooked up with Sylvie and gotten her pregnant.

She'd had a hard time reconciling the stranger who'd gotten Sylvie pregnant with the man she'd been steadily falling for over the past few days. But at least Cannon had been single. Her father had been married.

"It wasn't a one-night stand," Aidan said. "Marcus and Gabriel met in Austin when we went back for one of our fraternity brothers' wedding."

"Was Mother there, too?"

"No. Joyce was presenting a paper at a psychology conference in St. Louis. She and your father weren't getting along particularly well at the time. She wanted him to leave the police force and find a job where he didn't put his life on the line. He refused. You know your dad. He loved police work. I can't even imagine him sitting at a desk all day."

Nor could Brit—but an affair. Cheating on her mother and then bringing Brit home for her to raise. But he'd left Sylvie behind.

"I'm not making excuses for Marcus, Brit. He wouldn't want me to. He never made excuses for himself. He loved your mother in his own way. He always did right up until the day she died. But he loved Gabriel, too. He was different with her, more carefree. I swear I could always tell when he'd been with her."

"How long did the affair last?"

"Almost two years, until Gabriel became pregnant with you and Sylvie."

"Don't tell me he deserted a woman pregnant with his twin daughters?"

"No. She deserted him, before she even knew there were twins. The guilt got the better of her, I guess. She moved away and told him she never wanted to see him again, that she was going to give the baby up for adoption. Marcus took it hard. As hard as I've ever seen him take anything, and, believe me, we'd been through a lot together."

"But she didn't give Sylvie up—only me."

"That wasn't the original plan. Somehow your dad found out when she gave birth. He showed up at the hospital and once he saw you and

Sylvie he begged her to let him adopt both of you. But she had fallen in love with her babies, too, and changed her mind about adoption."

"But I was adopted."

"Your dad could be very persistent when he set his mind to it. And he definitely set his mind on raising you. He'd always wanted a big family. Joyce couldn't have children and wasn't sure she wanted a family. But somehow he talked her into the adoption without letting her know the truth."

"More lies."

"He was human. He had his faults. We all do, Brit. Your dad and I probably had a few more than our share. I'm not sure how the decision was made about which twin he'd adopt, but I do know that he loved you from the first time he held you in his arms. Joyce did, as well. Both of them loving you so much was what turned their marriage around."

"How can a marriage built on lies be great?"

"Because there was more there than lies. I didn't tell you this to turn you against your dad, Brit. I probably shouldn't have told you at all, but I felt terrible when Sylvie was killed. I know that you two might have been close had you been given the chance."

"Did you ever meet Sylvie?"

"Only once, a few months after her mother died. Gabrielle had told her the truth when she realized she wasn't going to make it. Sylvie paid me a visit. She questioned me about Marcus and you. She said she might look you up one day, but she wasn't ready yet. I figure wanting to meet you was what brought her to Houston."

"And to her death."

"She was traveling into someone else's past to find herself," Cannon said. "That's what she told me the night I met her. I don't know why it popped into my head right now, but it did and suddenly it makes sense."

"I wish I'd met her before she was killed," Brit said. "I wish I'd met Gabrielle. So sad to have a twin sister and a biological mother I never knew. Too bad my dad never thought of giving me that."

It was the first time she'd ever thought of him as less than perfect. Turned out he was just a man.

"If you're interested, you have a half brother, as well," Aidan said. "Gabriel and her new husband had a son. Sylvie said he's a navy SEAL and quite a hero."

"I've talked to him," Brit said. "I got his name after Sylvie was killed and gave him a call. He never knew about me," Brit said. "Perhaps I'll try to meet him in person one day."

Right now, she just wanted to go back to the Dry Gulch Ranch and Kimmie.

Like Sylvie, she needed to rescue her present from all the secrets of the past. What better way to start than by loving her adorable, completely innocent niece?

Learning the truth about her dad had opened her eyes to a lot of things. As for Cannon and his irresponsible one-night stands and the paternity test that he hoped would save him from the responsibility of parenthood, he could go back to his bulls.

How could she ever have thought she was falling in love with him?

IT WAS ALMOST ten o'clock by the time Brit and Cannon arrived back at the Dry Gulch. They'd stopped for dinner at a restaurant and then were delayed for another hour due to a wreck on the interstate.

The house was quiet and dark, but they had called earlier to let R.J. know they were retuning tonight. The door would be unlocked and their beds ready and waiting. Brit was more than ready to climb between the crisp white shirts and cuddle beneath the warm quilt.

Unfortunately, her enthusiasm for participating in a search for the perfect Christmas tree had vanished. Her heart felt heavy, her mind bogged down with learning the truth about the man she'd practically worshipped for all the years of her life.

Once inside the house, Cannon walked her to the guest room. He lingered at the door. "I hate seeing you so upset, Brit. Is there anything I can do to help? Offer a shoulder to cry on or use as a punching bag to vent your frustrations?" He trailed his fingers down her arm and tried to take her hand.

She pulled away. "I'll be fine. I just need a little time to absorb everything I learned about my father tonight."

"Why do I get the feeling you are taking your anger toward your father for mistakes he made years ago out on me?"

"I'm not."

"So why do you pull away when I touch you and won't even look at me when we talk? A few hours ago I was the knight on the white horse who'd ridden to your rescue. Now suddenly I'm the enemy."

"You aren't the enemy. You came through for me when I needed you, and I appreciate that. But I'm no longer suffering from a concussion and Melanie Crouch is behind bars. The urgency has passed. You can go back to your life. I can go back to mine."

"You make this sound like a business deal."

"Think of it as a release from a contract you never meant to sign. You don't have to stick around to wait on the results of the paternity test. The only tie you might have to Kimmie is biological, just like you said about your relationship to R.J. Well, you can walk away without even feeling guilty. If any sacrifices are to be made, I'll make them. I'll take care of Kimmie."

"Whoa. You're way off base. I didn't see any of this coming, I'll grant you that. But if Kimmie's my daughter, I'll take full responsibility for her. I don't know how yet, but I'll find a way. I've never shirked on an obligation."

"And Kimmie would be your obligation?"

"I didn't mean that the way it sounded. You're upset. I get that. Let's call it a night."

"First, satisfy my curiosity, Cannon. How many one-night stands have you had? How many women have you slept with that you don't even remember the next day?"

"So that's what this is about?"

"You didn't answer the question."

Anger flared in Cannon's eyes. "I don't intend to start explaining everything in my past life to you. But just for the record, I don't make a habit of getting drunk and picking up women in bars. I'm not saying I've never had a fling that was purely physical, but those times are few and far between."

"Yet you admit that's all you shared with Sylvie."

"I can't explain that night or what was going on in her mind. I'm not perfect. It's a foolproof bet she wasn't, either. Maybe she'd had the kind of day you had today or the kind I'd had that night. Maybe all either of us needed was a place to feel wanted and safe for a few hours."

"What kind of night does it take for you to make love to a woman you feel nothing for?"

"Okay, you want the truth. Here it is. It takes watching your best friend get his brains kicked out by a mad bull. It takes holding him in your arms while he breathes his last breath. It takes telling his wife who's expecting their first baby that he's never coming home again."

His voice dropped to a husky whisper, sadness replacing the anger in his eyes.

"I'm not your father, Brit. But it's awful easy for you to preach forgiveness and understanding when it applies to me and R.J. and then be quick to turn against your father, a man who never once stopped loving you."

Brit was trembling as Cannon turned and walked away.

Tears filled her eyes as she crossed the room

and dropped to the bed. Before she'd looked at a double of herself lying on that cold hard slab—before Kimmie and Cannon had dropped into her life—she'd known who she was and exactly what she wanted.

Now all her priorities had been scrambled beyond the point of recognition. Sylvie had been looking for her future in the past. But the past couldn't be changed. It couldn't be relived. It could only be learned from, the good cherished, the bad released.

Brit was about to throw her future away.

She jumped from the bed, rushed to the bathroom, washed her face and brushed her teeth. She shed her clothes and pulled on her robe.

Heart pounding, she raced down the hallway and up the stairs. She tapped at the first closed door.

Cannon opened it. He looked surprised but wary. "Is something wrong?"

"No. Everything is right—unless you don't want me."

"I'm not looking for a one-night pity stand, Brit."

"Good, because I'm thinking more like a new beginning with the option of indefinite. But I'm warning you, if you make love with me tonight, you are going to remember it for the rest of your life."

He opened his arms and she stepped inside them, sure of only one thing. There was no place she'd rather be than in his bed tonight.

BRIT AWAKENED TO mouthwatering smells wafting up from the kitchen and a gentle ache in her thighs. Deliciously sweet memories of making love to Cannon danced through her senses.

She rolled over to crawl back into his arms. He wasn't there. She did the next best thing and pulled his pillow against her naked breasts. Breasts that would never be the same after being massaged, nibbled and sucked by Cannon until she'd thought her nipples would become permanently erect and puckered.

The musky scent of Cannon and of their love-making still clung to the sheets and his pillow. She breathed it in, savoring it the way she had his every touch last night.

His fingers had explored every inch of her. His lips had teased and tasted until he'd driven her mad with wanting him.

When she'd reached the mind-blowing edge of orgasm, he'd trailed his probing tongue and ravishing lips back to her mouth and kissed her senseless.

And then he'd raised his beautiful naked body over hers and entered her with one heart-stopping thrust of his rock-hard erection. Both wild with desire, they'd ridden the wave of passion home.

Totally spent after that, she was certain it would take days of recovery before either of them would be able to make love like that again.

Two hours later, she'd been proven wrong. Now she wondered if she'd ever be able to get enough of his loving.

But it was morning and the Christmas Tree Search was waiting. She threw her legs over the side of the bed, padded across the room to the window and opened the blinds. Tiny white flakes of snow were falling from a slightly overcast sky.

It had to be a good omen.

She dressed quickly in jeans and a pullover sweater that wouldn't be too hot in the house but would provide a nice layer of warmth beneath her jacket. Her stylish leather riding boots didn't fit the cowboy tradition, but they would do just fine. It was going to be a beautiful day.

Excited voices, all seemingly talking at once, reached her ears the moment she opened her door. The wonderful family Cannon refused to be a part of. She hoped that would change—for his sake and Kimmie's.

And for hers. Who wouldn't want to be part of this family?

She couldn't imagine how Cannon's and her

jobs and lifestyles would mesh, but she wouldn't let herself worry about that now. Nor would she think of all the secrets Aidan had shared with her last night.

The day was rife with pleasure and anticipation. She'd let nothing spoil it.

CANNON HELPED ADAM arrange the warm quilts in the seat of the small horse-drawn carriage. "This is a beauty. Where did you get it?"

"On the property. It was in an old barn near the northwestern edge of the spread that hadn't been used in years. Leif, Travis, Cornell and I decided to tear down the barn. The carriage was buried under a stack of old pine logs."

"It must have taken a lot of work to restore it."

"It took some time, but well worth it. Lila and Lacy love going for a ride in what they call their Santa Claus carriage. The difference between sleigh and carriage is a still a little fuzzy with them."

"I heard how excited they were at breakfast."

Adam laughed. "I don't doubt that. They never go unnoticed. I missed the first three years of their lives and then almost lost them to a kidnapper. I know what they mean to me."

"They were kidnapped from the ranch?"

"No, from Hadley's mother's house in Dallas. It's a long story. I'll save it for a cold winter night. We'll get plenty of those in January and February. Right now you and the detective best get saddled up or the rest of the group will be hollering at you. The rules say we all leave at once and get back here in two hours."

"What's the prize?"

"The chance to have your tree in the family room at the big house. That's where we all gather for stories and songs before midnight church services on Christmas Eve and for opening gifts on Christmas morning."

"That sounds like a lot of togetherness."

"It is, but there's plenty of alone time on the Dry Gulch. Wide-open spaces. Best fishing and hunting in the county. Great swimming hole in the summer. I realize you have issues with R.J. We all did. We all had reason to. But you can't hang on to past hurts forever. The old resentments will eat you alive."

Interesting theory, but Cannon wasn't being eaten alive and he wasn't buying the theory.

"Guess I better get back to the tack room. I'm sure Brit is revved for riding."

He walked the few yards to where he had left everyone saddling their mounts for the morning ride. The horse barn was quiet and empty now. Well, almost empty.

R.J. finished washing his hands in water from a hose spout and wiped them on the legs of his baggy jeans. "I was wondering where you got off to."

"I was helping Adam ready the carriage."

"Good. Glad you got to spend some time with him. He's a good man. Knows more about life in his thirties than I ever learned."

Cannon didn't doubt that. "Have you seen Brit?"

"She left here a few minutes ago on Miss Dazzler. That's my special horse. Wouldn't let just anybody ride her, but I like Brit a lot."

"So do I." More than he'd ever imagined possible. "What horse do you want me to ride?"

"Raven. He's already saddled and ready to go, and waiting for you at the corral. That's the starting point for this competition Effie and Cornell are so excited about."

"I'd best head over there. Don't want to keep the crowd waiting."

"Won't kill 'em to wait another few minutes."

"You got something to say to me, R.J.?"

"Just need to get a couple of things off my chest."

"Let's hear them."

"I know I didn't do right by you. I wasn't there when your mother died, same as I wasn't there for Leif and Travis. But I did try to help out when I could get my hands on some money. There wasn't much of that back then."

"Hard to believe when there is supposedly millions now."

"I didn't lay it out in the will, but I've told the others so I might as well level with you. I didn't earn that money. Sure as hell didn't save it."

"So where did you get it?"

"I bought a one-dollar lottery ticket in Oak Grove. Damn thing hit the jackpot. Well, not one of those gigantic jackpots, but a few million after taxes was big-time for me. Went from poor rancher to millionaire overnight."

That explained a lot, though it didn't change Cannon's mind about the man.

"I sent what I could to your uncle to help pay your way when you were growing up, Cannon. I know it weren't much, but I paid for your braces like he asked me to. I borrowed and sent him the money for your medical expenses that time you fell out of the tree and broke your leg."

"You must have me mixed up with one of your other sons. I never had braces. I fell out of several trees, but I never broke any bones. You never sent me or my uncle as much as a birthday card."

R.J. shook his head. "I don't have my facts mixed up. If your uncle says differently he's a lying son of a bitch. Sorry to put it so bluntly, but that's the dadgum truth. You believe who you want. I can't do nothing about that. I just want you to know that there's a place for you and Kimmie here and I'd be mighty proud if you decided to move to the Dry Gulch."

No ready response came to mind. "I appreciate you and the rest of the family helping out with Kimmie." It was the only honest answer he could give without laying more guilt on a dying man.

THEY HAD TAKEN the horses to a trot and then a gallop, slowing again when the sting of the icy wind became more painful than the exhilaration.

Brit stuck out her tongue to catch a snowflake. "Just look around you, Cannon. The massive trunk and crooked branches of that ancient oak tree. The clear, rocky bottom of the shallow stream. The carpet of pine straw and crunchy leaves. I never dreamed the Dry Gulch would be this beautiful in the falling snow."

"Then enjoy. It won't last long. It's freezing this morning, but we're supposed to reach a high of thirty-seven this afternoon. It will all melt."

"But it's here now and beautiful. I love the way summer and fall tangle for control deep into the winter in this part of Texas."

"You seem to be loving everything today," he teased.

"Maybe because I had a great night."

"There's more where that came from."

"I'll hold you to that."

They rode side by side along the stream for twenty minutes or more and then detoured into the woods.

"You'd best start staking out the perfect tree," Cannon said. "We'll need to head back soon if we want to meet the deadline and get there before the hot cocoa and sugar cookies are all gone."

Brit scanned the area. "Do you have any idea how to get back?"

"Sure. Just follow the north star."

"It's daylight."

"I knew that sounded too simple to be true."

He was teasing. She should have known he'd been paying attention to the way they'd come while she'd just been enjoying the ride.

Now it was time for her to do her job. She scanned the area as they walked the horses down a winding trail that went right through the woods. A few minutes later they came to a clearing at the top of a hill.

And there it was. Standing alone. A beautiful evergreen. A trunk as straight as a fence post. Lots of branches laden with forest-green needles.

"That's it," Brit said, pointing to the tree. She dismounted and untied the bow from the loop around her belt. Cannon took her reins as she darted off to crown her chosen tree.

Cannon tethered the reins to a low-hanging branch of a sycamore tree and joined her.

"It's perfect," she declared as she secured the bow to the highest branch she could reach.

"Absolutely perfect."

Only Cannon's voice had grown husky and his eyes were on her instead of the tree. He took her in his arms and she melted into his kiss as the snowflakes fell in their silent wonderland.

If a moment could last forever, she'd choose this one.

The moment didn't last nearly long enough.

"Do we have to go back so soon?" she asked when Cannon pulled away.

"It's my phone. It's vibrating, but I can ignore it."

"We shouldn't. It could be important."

"Okay. Your call." He took the phone out of his pocket and looked at the display.

"It's the lab."

Chapter Eighteen

Emotions Cannon couldn't unravel crashed down on him. He hadn't expected them to call on a Saturday. The past few days had been the longhand version of eight seconds on the bull, a tangled mesh of fear and anxiety and passion. He wasn't ready for this.

But he couldn't postpone the truth.

"Hello."

"Is this Cannon J. Dalton?"

"It is."

"We have the results ready from your paternity testing. You can pick them up Monday through Friday during our regular office hours."

"Can't you just tell me over the phone?"

"Wait. Let me see if you specified that on your form."

He'd specified it. The wait seemed endless.

"Congratulations, Mr. Dalton. You're the father of Kimmie Marie Hamm."

The news hit like a bolt of lightning even though he'd thought he was prepared.

"Would you like me to mail the full written report or would you rather come in and pick it up?"

His emotions were spinning so wildly it took a few seconds to digest her question.

"Mail it to the Oak Grove address that I gave you."

He barely heard the rest of her spiel. He turned off his phone and dropped it into his pocket.

"I'm Kimmie's father, just like you said."

She slipped her hands into his. "Are you okay?"

He had to think about that for a moment. "Yeah. I'm okay. I'm not sure about Kimmie. I have no idea how to take care of her."

"Most new fathers don't. You'll learn."

"Are you going to teach me?"

"I'm as much a novice as you are. I realized that the week she stayed with me. But I'll help you all I can. So will your family. They already love her."

"I feel kind of like life as I know it has been ripped out from under me."

"It will definitely change," Brit said. "There will be lots of adjustments, but you'll make a wonderful father."

If he did, no one would be more surprised than him.

But strangely, he wasn't as upset as he'd expected to be. In fact, he had that same warmth creeping into his chest as he'd felt the first night he'd held Kimmie and she'd curled her tiny fingers around his.

"Shall we go back to the house and share the news?" Brit asked.

He managed a shaky smile. "I should have bought cigars."

THE REST OF Saturday and into Sunday morning had passed in a blur and a frenzy of celebration. You'd have thought he'd just won a Nobel Peace Prize instead of finding out that he was a father.

Cannon would be glad when the hoopla settled down. He had endless decisions to make about how to take care of an infant on the rodeo circuit. Maybe he should just kidnap R.J.'s grandmotherly-type neighbor Mattie Mae and take her with him.

It was eleven o'clock on Sunday morning and he and Brit were stuck in slow-moving traffic on the outer limits of Houston. His old doubts were returning at the speed of the jerk on the motorbike who'd just passed them on the shoulder.

"I'm not good with you staying in that town house alone."

"I live there, Cannon."

"Do you remember what it looked like the last time you were in it?"

"I remember vividly. It doesn't look that way now. I just talked to the cleaning service. The police tape is down and the place has been scrubbed so clean I'll think it's been renovated."

"I still don't think you should be alone until..."

"Until what? Every criminal in Houston is arrested and behind bars? That is never going to happen. If it did, I'd be out of a job."

"I could hire you as a nanny."

"I'd become a buckle bunny with a baby on my hip. That would be over-the-top disgusting."

"You could start a new trend."

She reached across the console and brushed her hand up and down his thigh.

"Plying me with sexual favors will not assuage my worry."

"I know you're afraid for me, Cannon. Police work and going after murderers is new for you. But it's what I do. I'm a detective. I handle investigations. It's not like I'm out chasing down killers every night."

"Clive Austin almost killed you."

"Clive Austin is dead and the woman who hired him is in jail and will be for a long, long, time."

She made sense. He knew that, but knowing and feeling were entirely different things.

Brit was convinced that Melanie was the one who'd schemed to kill her and killed Sylvie and Clive Austin in the process. But what if she was wrong? What if all the supposition and circumstantial evidence had led them to the wrong conclusion? Or what if Melanie had managed to hire another killer even before she'd sliced Clive's throat?

And what if he was going overboard with this? It would be as bad as if Brit was making decisions about his life, telling him to give up bull riding and get an office job.

The anxiety swelled again when he pulled onto her street and spotted a black sedan parked in Brit's driveway.

"Looks like you have company."

"Unexpected company," Brit said. "I don't recognize the vehicle."

Cannon parked his truck behind the car, blocking it in. He killed the engine and jumped out of the car to check things out. Brit, of course, was right behind him.

He recognized the driver immediately, despite the fact that her eyes were swollen and red, her mascara smeared and running down one cheek like black tears.

"Louise, what's wrong?" Brit asked.

"Aidan left me," she muttered between near hysterical sobs. "After you left last night, he got drunk and started calling me names. He said it was my fault he'd lost his job. My fault our son was in prison. I couldn't reason with him."

"I'm sure he's sobered up by now," Cannon offered. "He probably doesn't even remember what he said."

"He may be sober, but he hasn't been home since Friday night and he's not answering his phone. For all I know he's dead." The hysterics started again. "You have to help me get him back, Brit. You have to tell him it's not my fault. I can't live without Aidan. He's all I have."

"Let's go inside," Brit said. "I'll make some hot tea. We'll talk and figure out what to do."

Louise nodded, opened the door and practically fell out of the car. Cannon grabbed her arm for support.

"I've got it from here, Cannon," Brit assured him.

"Are you sure?"

"I'm sure. I'll call you later. Drive safely. I'll see you soon."

There was nothing left for him to do but drive away.

BRIT WAS TERRIBLE with handling hysterical women. She and Louise hadn't been close in years. Going to see Aidan Friday night may have been the biggest mistake in her life.

She led Louise through the front door of her town house and into her cozy living room. "Take this chair," Brit urged, tugging her to the most comfortable seat in the room. "Try to calm down. I'll heat some water for tea."

Once the tea bags were steeping in the hot water, Brit walked to the bedroom door and peered inside. All traces of the brutal attack had been scrubbed away just as her cleaning lady had promised. Still, an icy tremble climbed Brit's spine as thoughts of the horrid pictures filled her mind.

When the tea was ready, Brit put it on a tray and started back to the living room. Thankfully, Louise's body-racking sobs had grown silent. Perhaps now she'd listen to reason.

Aidan might have gotten drunk after their emotional talk the other night. Heaven knows, she'd felt like doing that herself, and she never drank to the point of intoxication. But Aidan and Louise had been through hell and back together. Brit couldn't believe he'd leave her now.

He'd be back. In the meantime, hysterics weren't going to help.

"Tea's ready," she said as she rejoined Louise.

"Thank you, bitch. Now sit it down and don't make another move."

Brit stared into Louise's cold, tearless eyes

and at the pistol she held with both hands. Panic rose in her throat.

She set the tray on an end table. "Put the gun down, Louise." She struggled to keep her voice low and reassuring. "I don't know what happened between you and Aidan, but it's not my fault. Killing me won't solve anything."

"It may not, but it will make me feel a whole lot better."

The hysterics had been an act. Louise had crossed the line between sanity and madness and somehow her anger had turned to Brit.

"I've never done anything to you, Louise. You must know that. You were almost like a second mother to me when I was growing up. I would have never hurt you."

"You didn't have to. Your father did enough for both of you. Pretending to be Aidan's best friend all those years. Expecting Aidan to keep his dirty little secrets while he destroyed our lives. You are just like him. You've always been just like him. Even at your prom, you lied and told your father my son was on drugs."

"My father never..."

Brit's words died as the truth suddenly hit home. It wasn't Melanie who had hired someone to kill her. It was Louise. The comment from Clive about her father made sense now.

But Melanie had Clive's phone number in her phone. Why? Unless ....

"You and Melanie Crouch were partners, weren't you? You pooled your money and hired Clive Austin to kill me."

"Dragging Melanie into this was all Clive's idea. When I refused to pay him what he wanted, he tried to persuade Melanie to pay him for the same job—double dipping so to speak. She refused. In the end the bumbling thug agreed to kill you for what I'd offered to pay him."

"Only instead of paying him, you slashed his throat."

"He was trash. The world is better off without him. The same way it's better off without your father."

The pieces were all falling into place. The nauseating truth swelled inside Brit's chest until she could barely breathe. "You hired someone to kill my father, didn't you? While Aidan was at the funeral crying with me, you must have been celebrating your success."

"Marcus deserved it. He destroyed my husband and my son. He tore our family apart. I swore to wipe out his family the way he did mine. That's why you have to die, Brit. It's why Sylvie had to die."

"No one else needs to die, Louise. You've

taken enough revenge. Think about what you're doing. Stop the killing."

"I will, after you're dead. You're the last one. I've run out of money. That's why I have to kill you myself. Strange how much I'm looking forward to it. Once you're dead, maybe I can sleep at night."

Louise was mad, far past reasoning. Brit had to find a way to stop her. "You won't get away with this, Louise."

"Oh, but I will. Thanks to you, Melanie is already in jail for hiring Clive Austin to kill you. When they find you dead, they'll be convinced she hired someone else to kill you. Case solved."

"Cannon knows you were here when he left, Louise. If you pull that trigger, he'll know it was you who killed me."

"Cannon saw me in tears, weeping over an argument with my husband. An argument I staged and pushed until Aidan walked out on me. He's done it before. He always comes back. He's a good man, not a cheat like your father."

"Hand me the gun, Louise. We were so close once. You don't want to kill me."

"I have to kill you. You must see that. But you're lucky, Brit. It will all be over for you in a matter of seconds. You can't imagine how many nights I've cried myself to sleep, praying that I would never wake up."

No. She couldn't die. Not like this. She had to be there for Kimmie. She had to tell Cannon how much she loved him.

Brit scanned the room, looking for a distraction, a weapon, for anything to give her a fighting chance.

She lurched for the heavy glass lamp and hurled it at Louise just as she pulled the trigger. The bullet hit the lamp. Sharp shards of glass rained down on them. Louise howled and grabbed her right eye. Still, she kept coming at Brit, one eye bloody, the other open, the pistol poised to shoot.

I love you, Cannon and sweet Kimmie, I love you so much. I don't want to lose you. This is not the way this was supposed to end.

Chapter Nineteen

Cannon stopped for gas one block from the entrance to I-45 North. He still couldn't shake the unwanted anxiety or get the case against Melanie Crouch out of his mind. He agreed she was a suspect and should be in jail, but there were far too many assumptions for him to fully buy her guilt.

And too many unanswered questions. Why bury your wedding album for symbolic closure if you were still holding a murderous grudge against the cop who arrested you for killing him? Why waste your money on hiring a killer instead of using it to support you in paradise for the rest of your life?

And then there was the comment tying the attempted murder to Brit's father. From what he'd heard, there were no apparent ties between Clive Austin or Melanie Crouch and Chief of Police Marcus Garner. No reason to suspect Melanie knew Sylvie was Brit's sister.

They should be looking for someone like Louise McIntosh, who hated Brit's father and knew the truth about Sylvie and Brit's relationship.

Someone like Louise.

Truth hit with the force of a hatchet, the blade landing right in the center of Cannon's heart. He jerked the gas hose from his tank, jumped in his truck and took off. Someone yelled at him from the service station. They could damn well stick the hose back in the pump themselves. If his fears were right, every second counted.

He turned the corner on squealing wheels as adrenaline rushed through his veins. Louise's car was still parked in the driveway.

For once he prayed his instincts were all wrong, that Brit and Louise were having tea and talking about the rotten way Aidan had treated his wife. The praying didn't stop the grinding fear in the pit of his stomach.

His tires screeched as he swerved into the driveway and stamped on his brakes. He grabbed his pistol, bounded from the truck and raced to the door, prepared to shoot off the lock if it came to that.

His hand was on the doorknob when he heard the booming crack of gunshot followed by a piercing scream. Choking panic balled like acid in his throat.

He turned the doorknob and pushed through the front door, his weapon poised to shoot. A chair came flying at him; he ducked just as he saw Brit pounce on Louise and knock her to the floor.

Brit shoved a glass paperweight into Louise's face. But Louise kicked and managed to get away just long enough to reach for a gun she must have lost in the scuffle. Before Cannon could stop her, Louise's finger closed around the trigger.

He jumped over an overturned table and wrestled the pistol from her hand a heartbeat after she fired. Blood shot into the air like an eruption.

Louise fell back to the floor, a pool of crimson blood already pooling on her shirt.

Cannon stepped over her and dropped to the floor next to Brit. "Are you all right?"

"All but my pride, but poor Louise. She's bleeding badly, Cannon. You have to help her."

Before he could, four armed cops crashed into the room, weapons pulled. One looked at Brit and then aimed his gun at Cannon's head.

"Police Officer. Guns down," Brit ordered. "Suspect down and injured. Cannon and I are unhurt."

A police officer she recognized stared at her. "Detective Garner?"

"Right," she said. "I was attacked, but not shot. I think the suspect was hit by her own ricocheting bullet."

One cop called for an ambulance. Another checked Louise's pulse and tried to stop her bleeding.

The officer she knew crossed the room to stand over Brit. "You sure you're all right, Detective Garner?"

"I am, Officer Cormier, thanks to my friend Cannon. If he hadn't arrived when he did, I'd be dead."

"How did you guys get here so fast?" Cannon questioned. "I didn't even get a chance to call you."

"The detective's got good neighbors. They called when they said a suspicious car was parked in her driveway. We heard a shot as soon as we drove up."

"Good work."

Cannon gave Brit a hand, tugged her to her feet and pulled her into his arms. "Am I going to have to spend the rest of my life rescuing you?"

"Do you have something better to do, cowboy?"

"Yeah, I do. I'll tell you about it as soon as we're alone. But don't worry, I'll always have your back."

She stretched to her tiptoes and put her lips to his ear. "Why stop with my back? You can have all of me."

That was a promise he planned to hold her to for the rest of their lives.

Epilogue

New Year's Day at the Dry Gulch Ranch

R.J. sat on the front porch swing, watching the action as the Dalton women scurried in and out of the house like ants.

"Are we expecting the Texas Army National Guard at this picnic?" he asked as Hadley passed with a four-layer chocolate cake.

"No, just half the neighbors in Oak Grove. It's a triple celebration. Don't want to leave anyone out."

"Triple. What more is there than New Year's?"

"You'll see."

Leif and Cannon pulled up in Cannon's pickup truck and started unloading yet another picnic table from the bed of the truck.

"Did you guys buy out the local hardware shop?"

"Nope, all borrowed," Leif called.

And they'd all be needed. When folks around

Oak Grove came to a picnic, none came empty-handed. They'd end up with enough food to stock the biggest restaurant chain in Texas.

Once the table was unloaded, Cannon climbed the steps to the porch and poured himself a glass of cold lemonade that Joni had brought out from the kitchen not five minutes ago.

"Real nice to have you and Kimmie here for the day," R.J. said.

"Glad to be here," Cannon said.

"How's it going trying to take care of her and keep up with the circuit?"

"It has its challenges, but I'm making it—for now."

"Good to hear. What's the latest on Louise McIntosh?"

"She's still in the hospital being treated for complications with her chest injury. Her physical situation is improving but her mental condition is deteriorating."

"I hear hate and resentment can do that to you if you hold on to it long enough. Seems there are lots of ways to ruin your life. I'm just lucky I got a second chance at happiness, however long that chance turns out to be."

"On that topic, I've got something I'd like to talk to you about."

"I'm nothing but ears."

R.J. listened to Cannon's plans, his heart

warming at every word out of Cannon's mouth. If he kept it up, the light jacket Faith had insisted he wear on this incredibly sunny day would start suffocating him.

"I don't see how that would be a problem," R.J. said. "This spread's big enough you can easily carve out a section to breed and raise rodeo stock. Build a place of your own like the others have or move into the big house with me. Lord knows there's room, and I'd appreciate the company."

"I'm just in the thinking stages."

"I understand that, too. Is Brit included in this thinking?"

"She's a major part of it."

"How does she feel about that?"

"I haven't asked her. I'm almost scared to. Her life's in Houston. She seems to like it that way."

"Likes and dislikes change like the seasons. Even Kimmie opened her mouth for pureed bananas this morning."

"You got a point. Now I better get back to work before the guys come looking for me."

R.J. leaned back in the swing and smiled. It would be plum dandy to have Cannon and Kimmie move onto the ranch. But a man needed a woman.

He closed his eyes and pictured a young lady

with hair the color of fresh-mowed hay and a smile that had made him melt just to look at.

His first love. Still alive, or so he'd heard a month or two ago. He wondered what she was doing today and if she still liked double-dip ice-cream cones.

A few minutes later he was snoring away and Gwen was dancing barefoot through his dream.

By SUNSET THE last of the guests had packed up their picnic baskets and headed back to their own farms and ranches.

Cannon's plans were all in place.

Kimmie was spending the night with Hadley and Adam, much to the delight of her four-year-old cousins, Lacy and Lila. The champagne was iced and waiting. Adam had just hitched the ranch's two most dependable geldings to the carriage. The quilts were folded and waiting.

And Cannon was so nervous it took three times to zip his jacket.

He went looking for Brit and found her standing on the porch looking up at the heaven full of stars.

"It was a perfect day," she said. "I loved it when Joni and Leif stood up and announced together that there would be a new Dalton arriving in six months. That bought a few whoops and hollers from the crowd."

"The Dalton clan is definitely growing," Cannon agreed.

"My very favorite moments were when you and the rest of your half brothers all stood and gave your special toasts to R.J."

"I don't think any of us expected he'd break down and cry," Cannon said.

"There were a lot of tears in that crowd. I was one of the ones who wept to see him so touched and to see you be a part of it. You've come a long way in a short time, Cannon. I'm so proud of you."

"I still have a ways to go. How about taking a moonlit ride with me?"

"In your truck?"

"In the carriage?"

"Just the two of us?"

"Did you want someone else?"

"No. Just you."

A few minutes later they arrived at Cannon's favorite place on the whole spread. A hilltop that looked down on a curve in the creek and acres of rolling pastureland.

He slowed the horses to a stop, reached in his pocket and wrapped his fingers around the tiny ring box. He'd mentally prepared himself all day to hear the word *no* from her lips, but now that he was about to pop the question, he couldn't deny how desperately he wanted Brit to say yes.

Holding the reins in one hand, he put his other arm around her shoulder and pulled her close. "I love you, Brit Garner. I love you so much I can't even think straight anymore."

"I love you, too, Cannon Dalton, so much that I am finally thinking straight. For the first time in my life, I know who I am and what I want."

"What do you want?"

"I want stars over my head and to be surrounded by laughter and love the way we were today. I want to be part of a family like the Daltons who laugh and cry together, who have their own interests and passions but are always there for one another, too. I want to spend lots and lots of time with Kimmie."

"Is that it?"

"No, I want love in my heart, passion in my soul and joy in the morning. I want you, Cannon Dalton. I love you so very, very much."

"Then I guess it's time for this."

He got down on one knee in the carriage and pulled the ring from his pocket. "Will you marry me, Brit Garner? I promise not to wear my boots to bed or make you go to rodeos, and not to come home with a hair on my shoulder that doesn't match my horse's mane. I promise to always give you the best eight seconds of my day."

"You've got yourself a deal, cowboy."

"What about the HPD?"

"They'll just have to learn to get along without me. I gave them my all while I was with them. Now I plan to be far too busy loving you and taking care of Kimmie, at least for now. That's not to say I might not talk Sheriff Garcia into hiring me one day in the future."

"I can live with that."

Cannon pulled her into his arms and when he touched his lips to hers, she knew she was home to stay.

Their pasts had shaped them and the good and the bad would always be part of them. But their love would guide their future. It would be one ecstatically glorious ride.

* * * * *